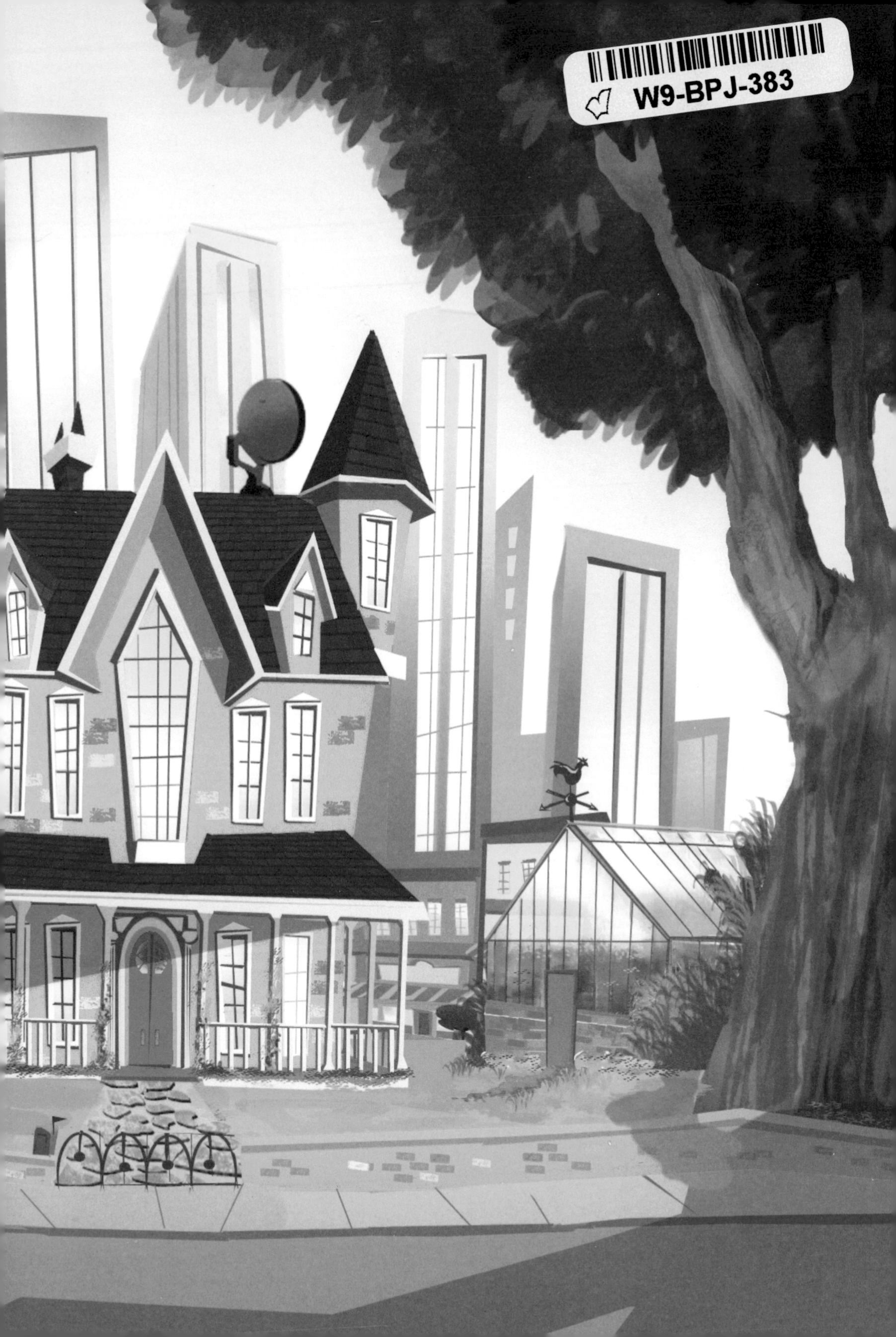

Geronimo Stilton™
Reporter

PAPERCUTZ™

Geronimo Stilton

GRAPHIC NOVELS AVAILABLE FROM PAPERCUTZ™

...ALSO AVAILABLE WHEREVER E-BOOKS ARE SOLD!

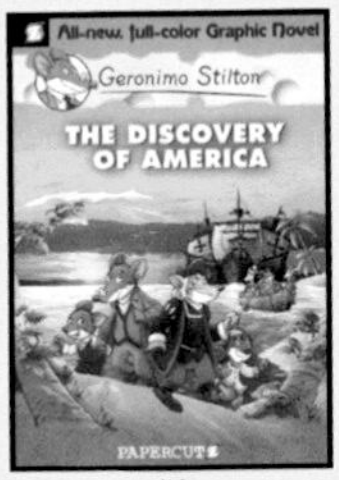
All-new, full-color Graphic Novel
Geronimo Stilton
THE DISCOVERY OF AMERICA
PAPERCUTZ

#1
"The Discovery of America"

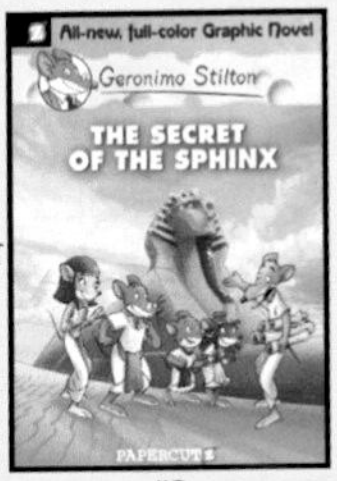
All-new, full-color Graphic Novel
Geronimo Stilton
THE SECRET OF THE SPHINX
PAPERCUTZ

#2
"The Secret of the Sphinx"

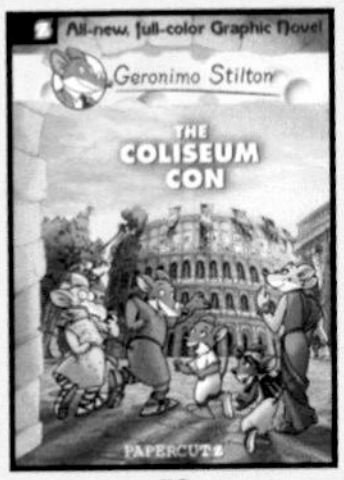
All-new, full-color Graphic Novel
Geronimo Stilton
THE COLISEUM CON
PAPERCUTZ

#3
"The Coliseum Con"

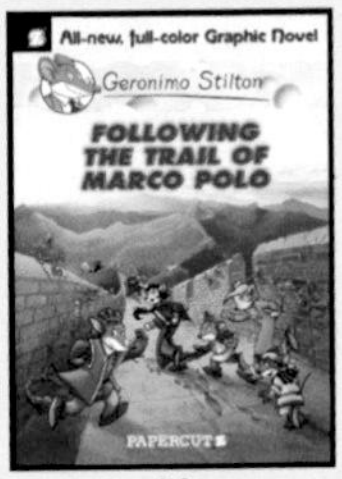
All-new, full-color Graphic Novel
Geronimo Stilton
FOLLOWING THE TRAIL OF MARCO POLO
PAPERCUTZ

#4
"Following the Trail of Marco Polo"

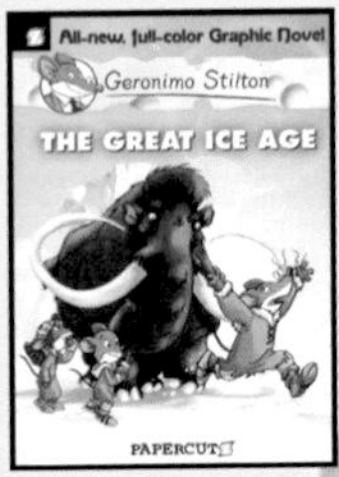
All-new, full-color Graphic Novel
Geronimo Stilton
THE GREAT ICE AGE
PAPERCUTZ

#5
"The Great Ice Age"

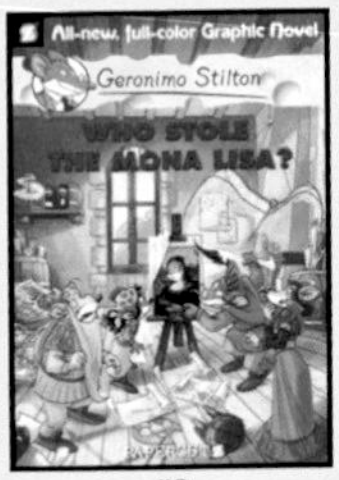
All-new, full-color Graphic Novel
Geronimo Stilton
WHO STOLE THE MONA LISA?

#6
"Who Stole the Mona Lisa?"

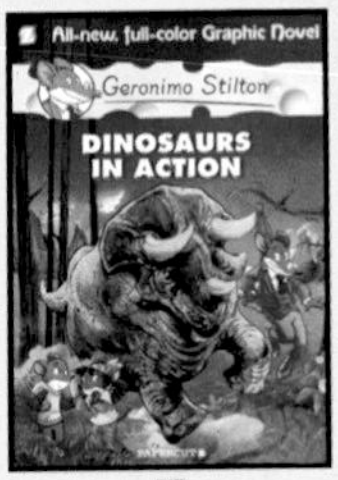
All-new, full-color Graphic Novel
Geronimo Stilton
DINOSAURS IN ACTION

#7
"Dinosaurs in Action"

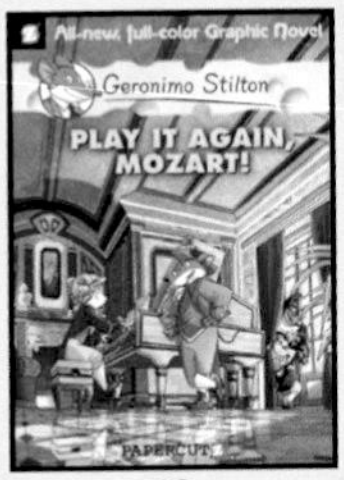
All-new, full-color Graphic Novel
Geronimo Stilton
PLAY IT AGAIN, MOZART!
PAPERCUTZ

#8
"Play It Again, Mozart!"

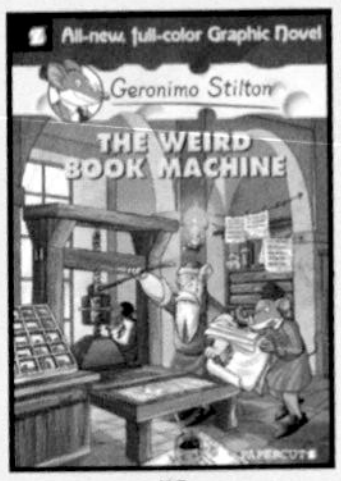
All-new, full-color Graphic Novel
Geronimo Stilton
THE WEIRD BOOK MACHINE
PAPERCUTZ

#9
"The Weird Book Machine"

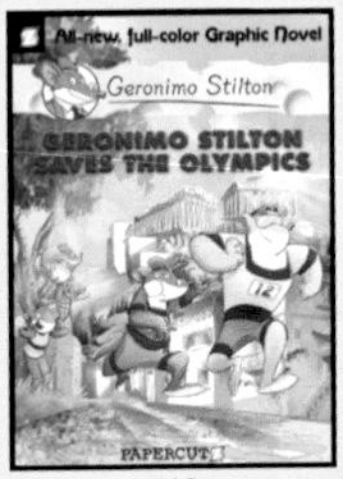
All-new, full-color Graphic Novel
Geronimo Stilton
GERONIMO STILTON SAVES THE OLYMPICS
PAPERCUTZ

#10
"Geronimo Stilton Saves the Olympics"

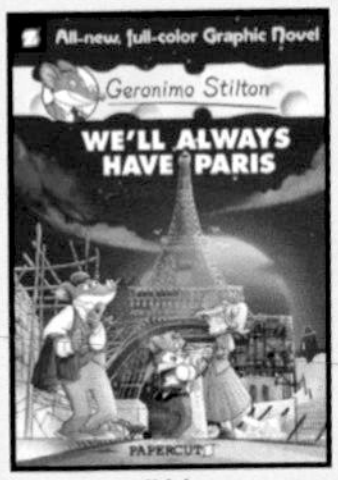
All-new, full-color Graphic Novel
Geronimo Stilton
WE'LL ALWAYS HAVE PARIS
PAPERCUTZ

#11
"We'll Always Have Paris"

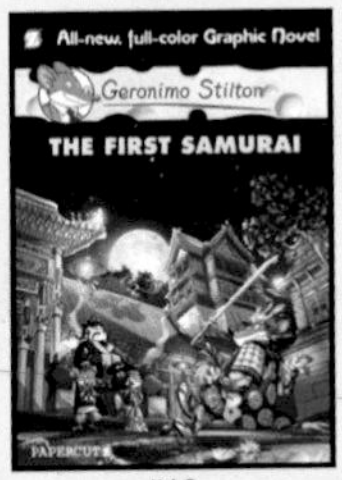
All-new, full-color Graphic Novel
Geronimo Stilton
THE FIRST SAMURAI
PAPERCUTZ

#12
"The First Samurai"

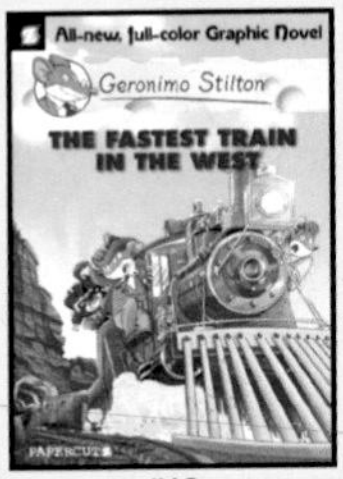
All-new, full-color Graphic Novel
Geronimo Stilton
THE FASTEST TRAIN IN THE WEST
PAPERCUTZ

#13
"The Fastest Train in the West"

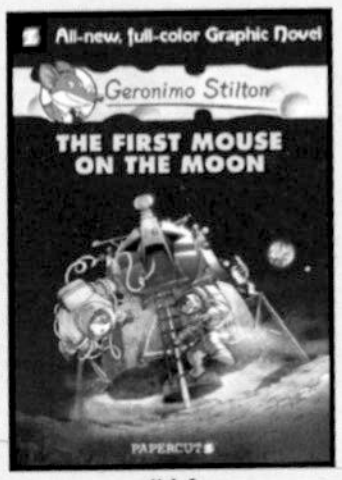
All-new, full-color Graphic Novel
Geronimo Stilton
THE FIRST MOUSE ON THE MOON
PAPERCUTZ

#14
"The First Mouse on the Moon"

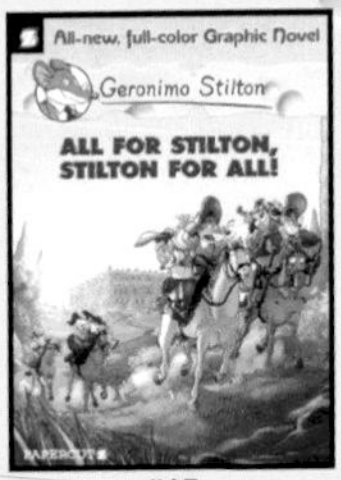
All-new, full-color Graphic Novel
Geronimo Stilton
ALL FOR STILTON, STILTON FOR ALL!
PAPERCUTZ

#15
"All for Stilton, Stilton for All!"

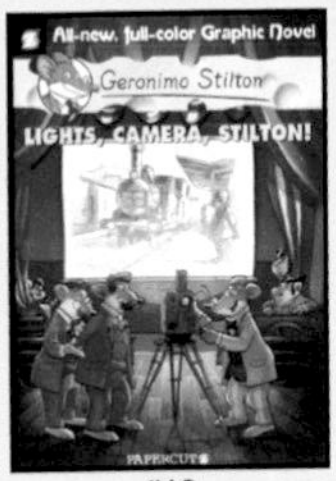
All-new, full-color Graphic Novel
Geronimo Stilton
LIGHTS, CAMERA, STILTON!
PAPERCUTZ

#16
"Lights, Camera, Stilton!"

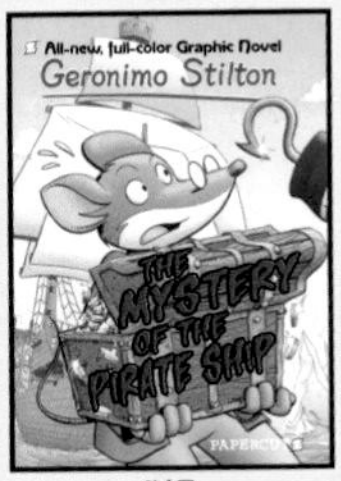
All-new, full-color Graphic Novel
Geronimo Stilton
THE MYSTERY OF THE PIRATE SHIP
PAPERCUTZ

#17
"The Mystery of the Pirate Ship"

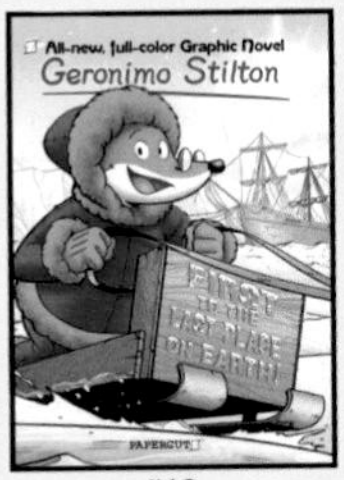
All-new, full-color Graphic Novel
Geronimo Stilton
PAPERCUTZ

#18
"First to the Last Place on Earth"

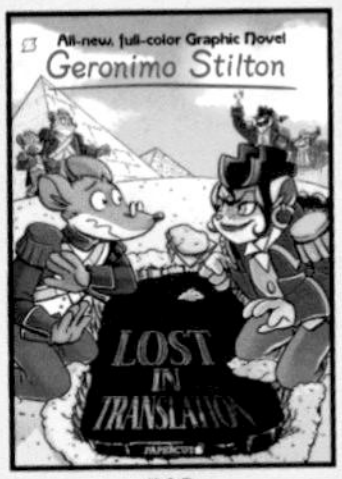
All-new, full-color Graphic Novel
Geronimo Stilton
LOST IN TRANSLATION
PAPERCUTZ

#19
"Lost in Translation"

GERONIMO STILTON graphic novels are available for $9.99 each only in hardcover. Available from booksellers everywhere. You can also order online from papercutz.com. Or call 1-800-886-1223, Monday through Friday, 9 – 5 EST. MC, Visa, and AmEx accepted. To order by mail, please add $5.00 for postage and handling for first book ordered, $1.00 for each additional book and make check payable to NBM Publishing. Send to: Papercutz, 160 Broadway, Suite 700, East Wing, New York, NY 10038.

Geronimo Stilton™ Reporter

#1 OPERATION SHUFONGFONG
By Geronimo Stilton

PAPERCUTZ™
NEW YORK

OPERATION SHUFONGFONG

Text by Geronimo Stilton
Cover by Alessandro Muscillo (artist) and Christian Aliprandi (colorist)
Editorial supervision by Alessandra Berello (Atlantyca S.p.A.)
Editing by Lisa Capiotto (Atlantyca S.p.A.)
Script by Dario Sicchio based on the episode by Vincent Bonjour and Julien Frey
Art by Alessandro Muscillo
Color by Christian Aliprandi
Original Lettering by Maria Letizia Mirabella

Based on an original idea by Elisabetta Dami
Based on episode 1 of the Geronimo Stilton animated series "Operazione Shufongfong."

www.geronimostilton.com

DAWN GUZZO—Production, Lettering
GRANT FREDERICK—Editorial Intern
JEFF WHITMAN—Assistant Managing Editor
JIM SALICRUP
Editor-in-Chief

ISBN: 978-1-62991-871-6

Printed in China
October 2018

Papercutz books may be purchased for business or promotional use.
For information on bulk purchases please contact Macmillan Corporate and Premium Sales
Department at (800) 221-7945x5442.

Distributed by Macmillan
First Printing

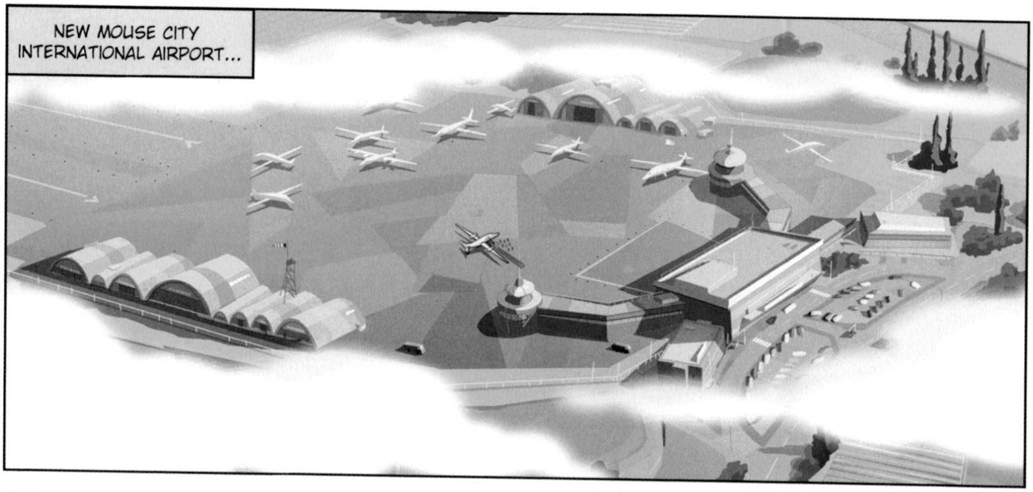
NEW MOUSE CITY INTERNATIONAL AIRPORT...

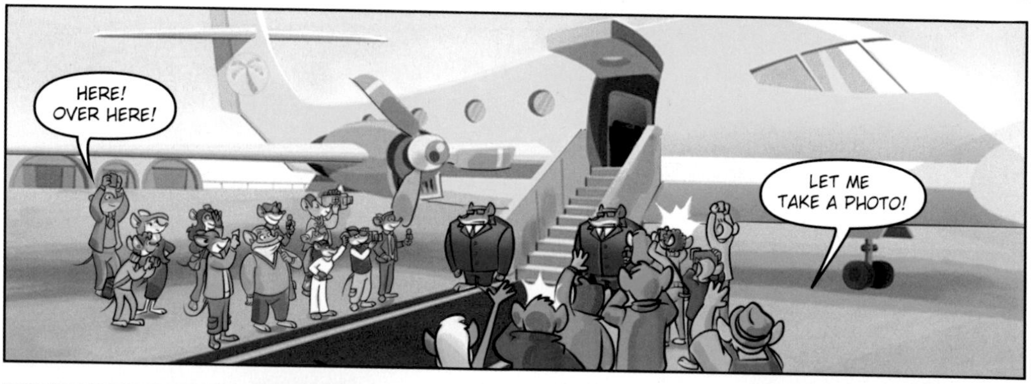
HERE! OVER HERE!
LET ME TAKE A PHOTO!

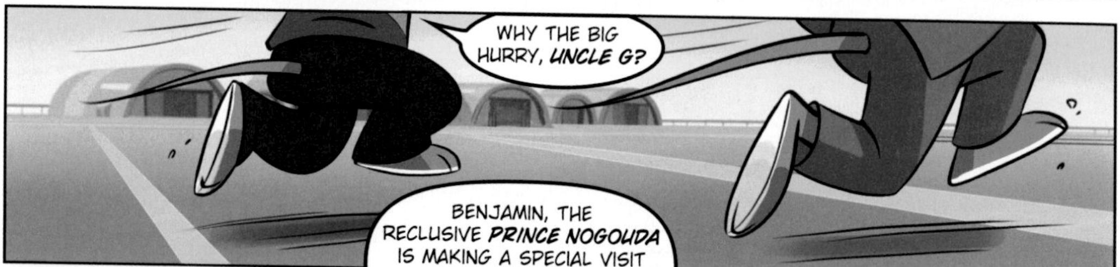
WHY THE BIG HURRY, **UNCLE G?**
BENJAMIN, THE RECLUSIVE **PRINCE NOGOUDA** IS MAKING A SPECIAL VISIT TO NEW MOUSE CITY AND I INTEND ON GETTING AN INTERVIEW!

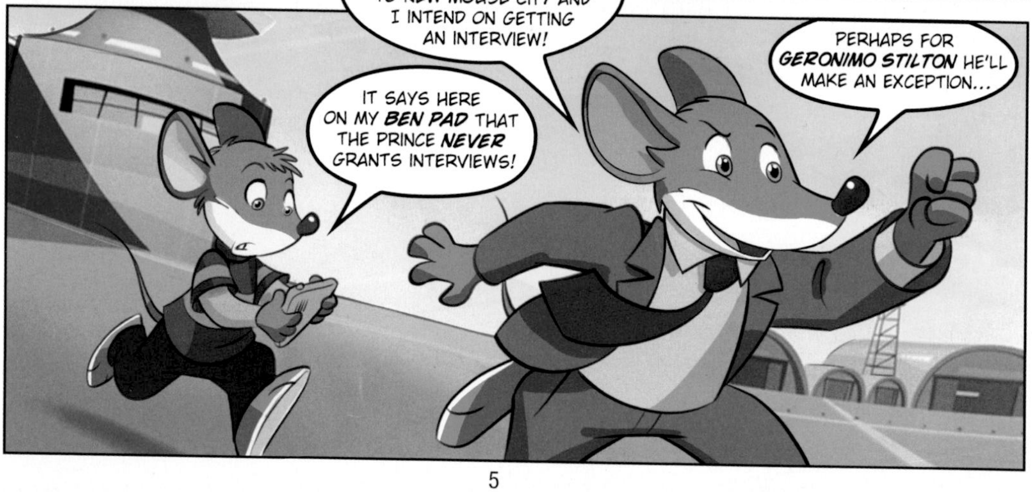
IT SAYS HERE ON MY **BEN PAD** THAT THE PRINCE **NEVER** GRANTS INTERVIEWS!
PERHAPS FOR **GERONIMO STILTON** HE'LL MAKE AN EXCEPTION...

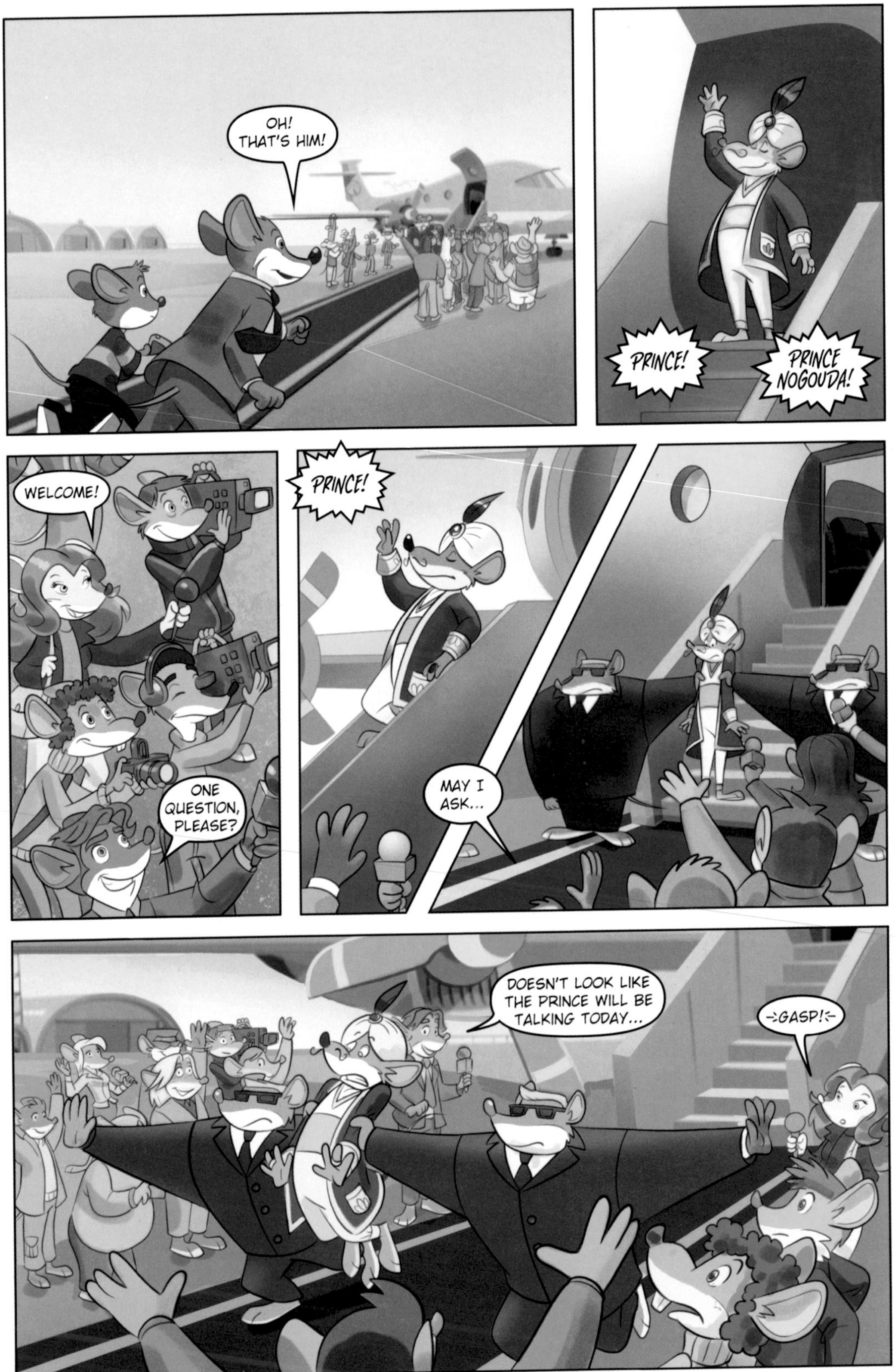
OH! THAT'S HIM!
PRINCE!
PRINCE NOGOUDA!
WELCOME!
ONE QUESTION, PLEASE?
PRINCE!
MAY I ASK...
DOESN'T LOOK LIKE THE PRINCE WILL BE TALKING TODAY...
-GASP!-

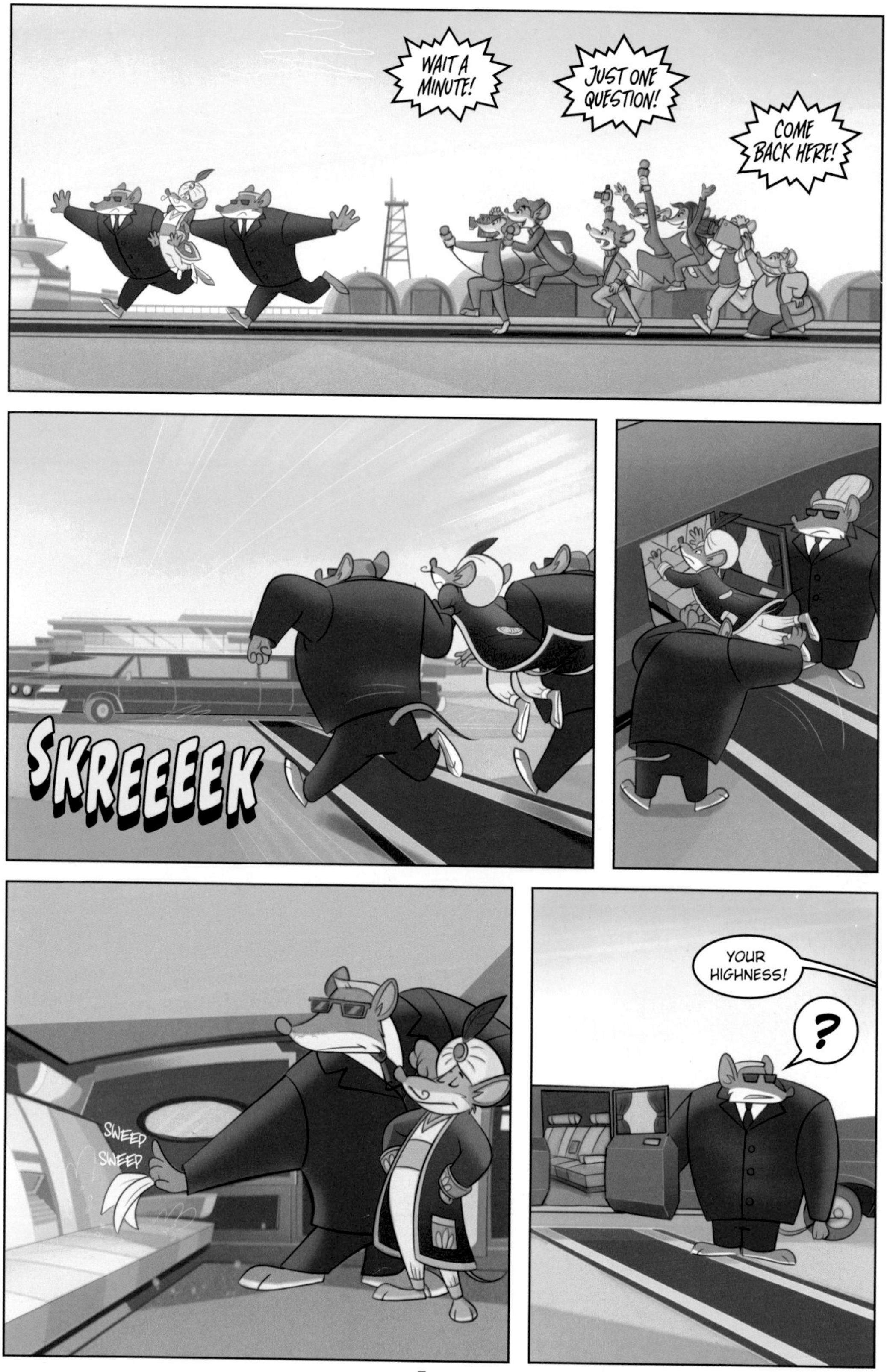
WAIT A MINUTE!
JUST ONE QUESTION!
COME BACK HERE!
SKREEEEK
SWEEP SWEEP
YOUR HIGHNESS!
?

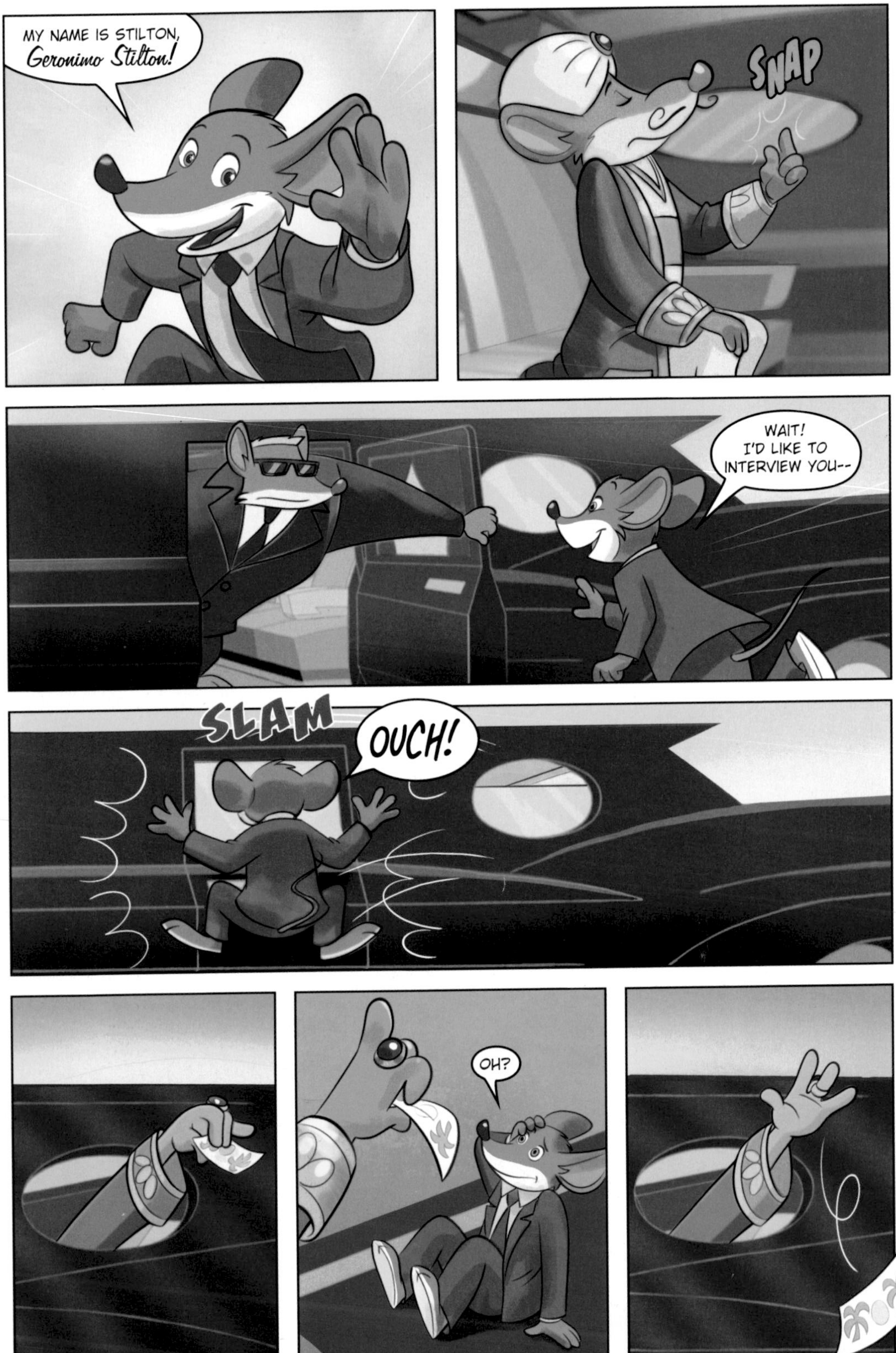
MY NAME IS STILTON, Geronimo Stilton!
SNAP
WAIT! I'D LIKE TO INTERVIEW YOU--
SLAM
OUCH!
OH?

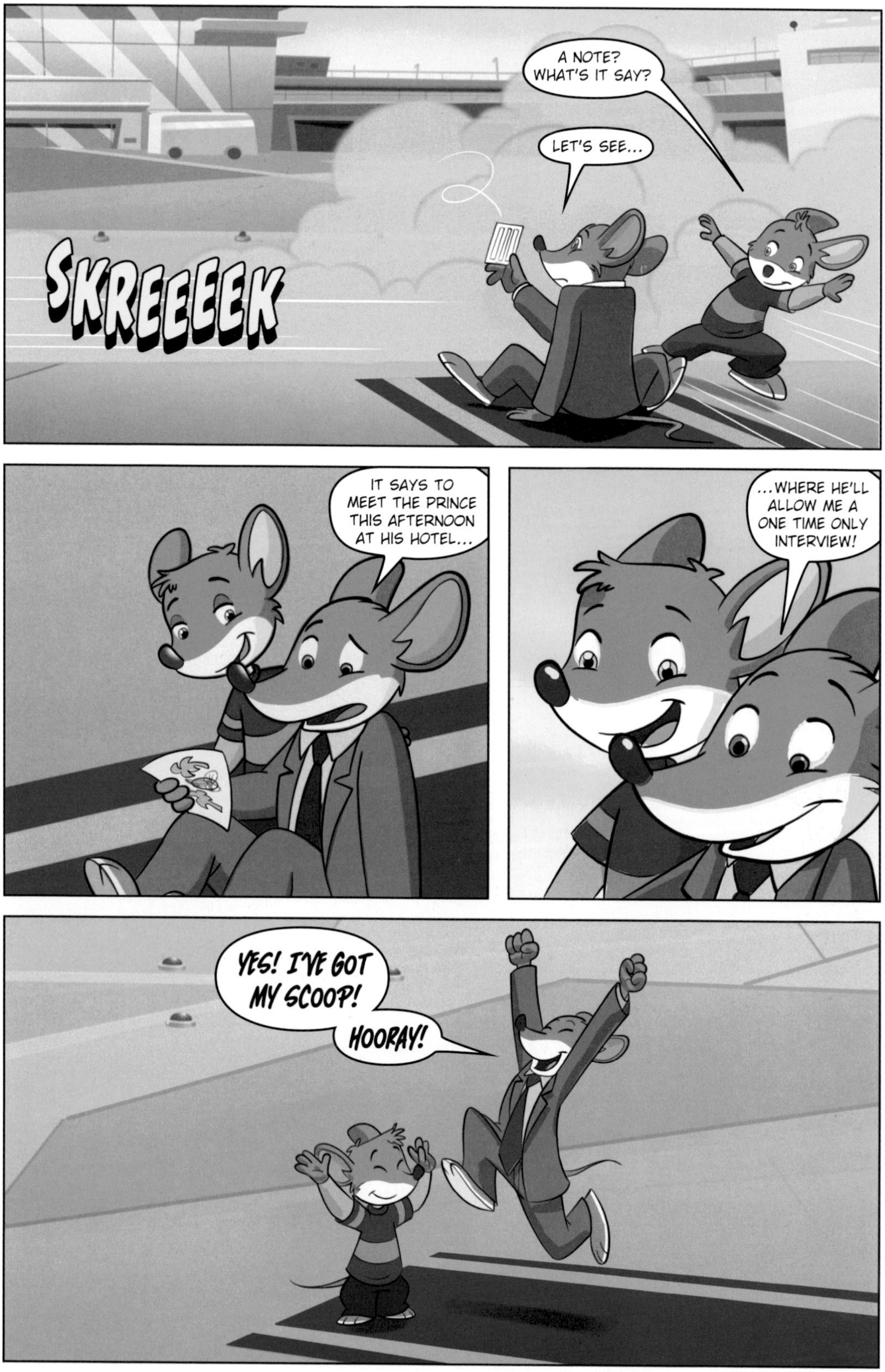
A NOTE? WHAT'S IT SAY?
LET'S SEE...
SKREEEEK
IT SAYS TO MEET THE PRINCE THIS AFTERNOON AT HIS HOTEL...
...WHERE HE'LL ALLOW ME A ONE TIME ONLY INTERVIEW!
YES! I'VE GOT MY SCOOP!
HOORAY!

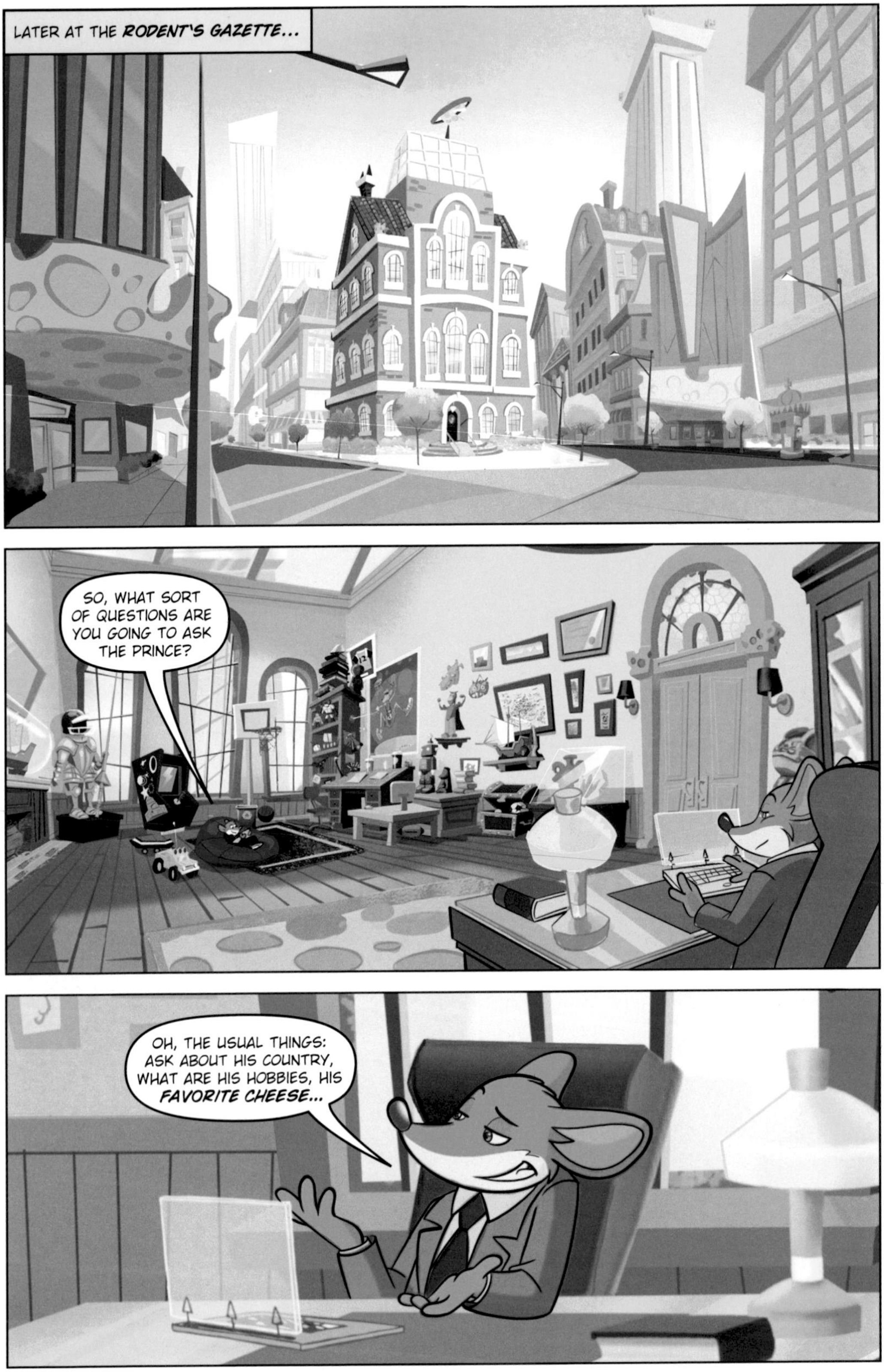
LATER AT THE **RODENT'S GAZETTE...**
SO, WHAT SORT OF QUESTIONS ARE YOU GOING TO ASK THE PRINCE?
OH, THE USUAL THINGS: ASK ABOUT HIS COUNTRY, WHAT ARE HIS HOBBIES, HIS **FAVORITE CHEESE...**

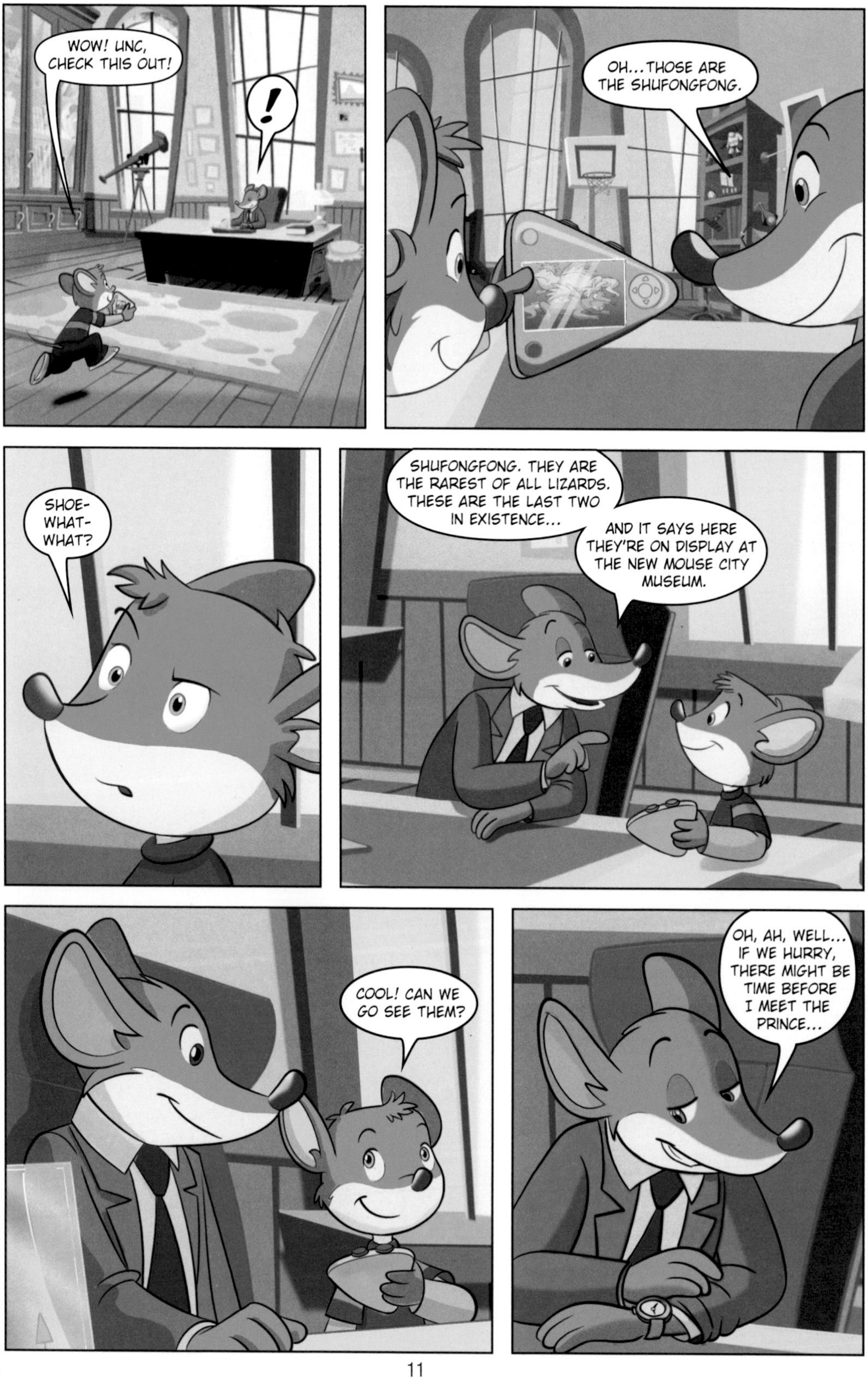
WOW! UNC, CHECK THIS OUT!
!
OH...THOSE ARE THE SHUFONGFONG.
SHOE-WHAT-WHAT?
SHUFONGFONG. THEY ARE THE RAREST OF ALL LIZARDS. THESE ARE THE LAST TWO IN EXISTENCE...
AND IT SAYS HERE THEY'RE ON DISPLAY AT THE NEW MOUSE CITY MUSEUM.
COOL! CAN WE GO SEE THEM?
OH, AH, WELL... IF WE HURRY, THERE MIGHT BE TIME BEFORE I MEET THE PRINCE...

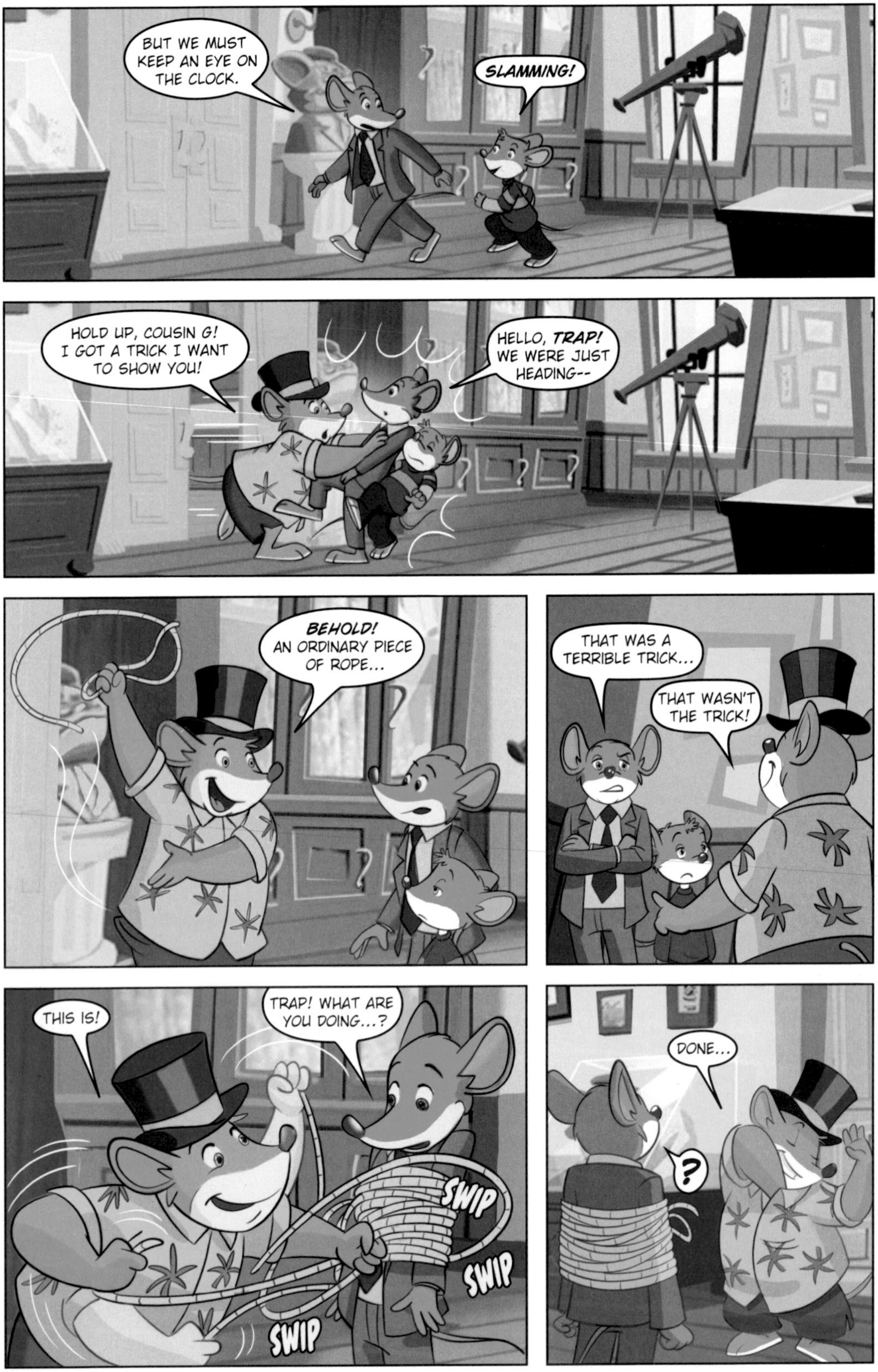
BUT WE MUST KEEP AN EYE ON THE CLOCK.
SLAMMING!
HOLD UP, COUSIN G! I GOT A TRICK I WANT TO SHOW YOU!
HELLO, TRAP! WE WERE JUST HEADING--
BEHOLD! AN ORDINARY PIECE OF ROPE...
THAT WAS A TERRIBLE TRICK...
THAT WASN'T THE TRICK!
THIS IS!
TRAP! WHAT ARE YOU DOING...?
SWIP
SWIP
SWIP
DONE...
?

AND NOW, I WILL MAKE THE KNOT DISAPPEAR!

POFF

SWEET!

OKAY, GREAT TRICK. NOW, UNTIE ME...

ONE WHISKER OF A PROBLEM... I HAVEN'T LEARNED HOW TO MAKE THE KNOT APPEAR AGAIN!

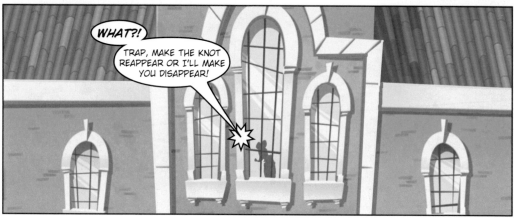

WHAT?!

TRAP, MAKE THE KNOT REAPPEAR OR I'LL MAKE YOU DISAPPEAR!

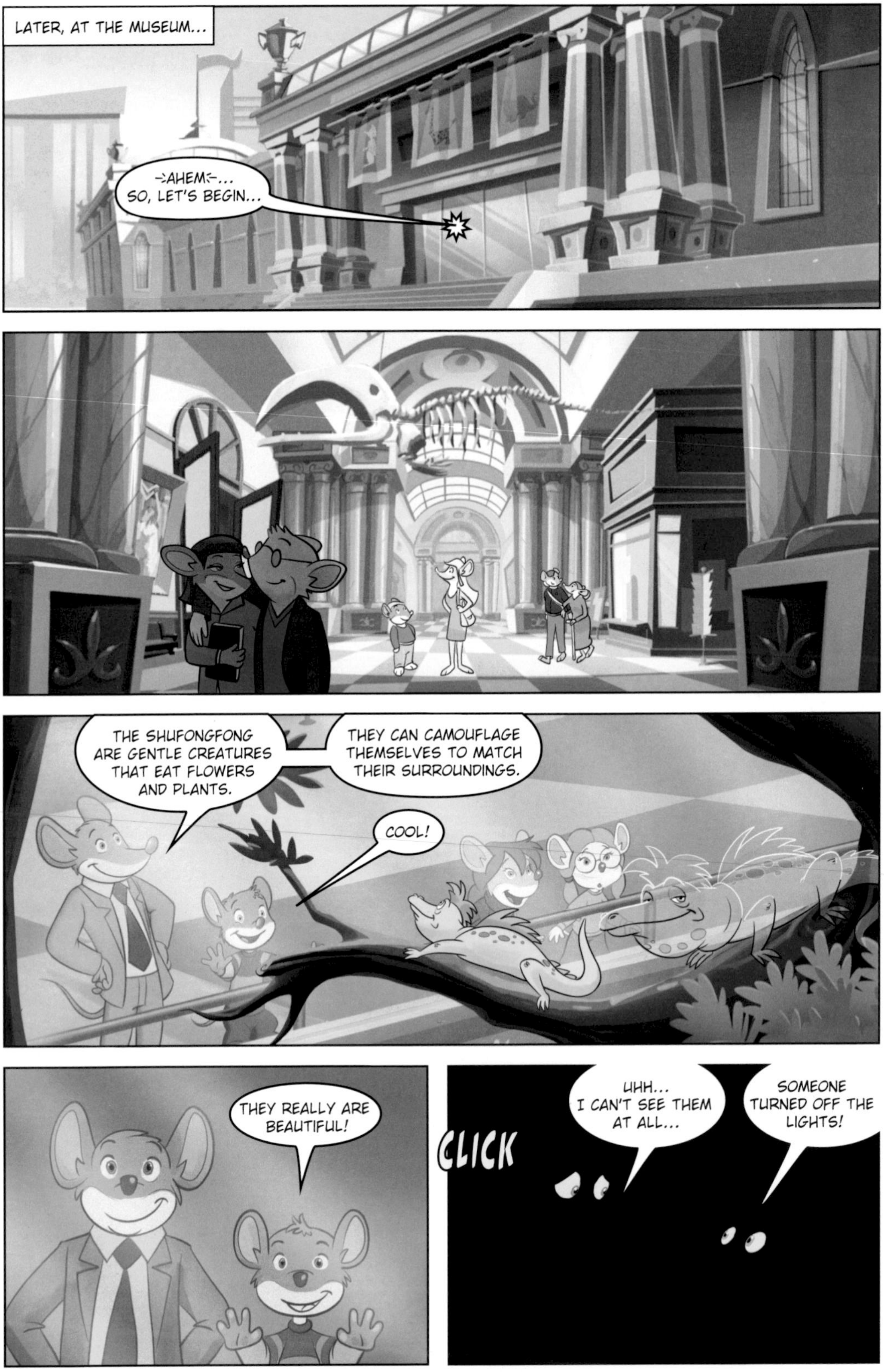
LATER, AT THE MUSEUM...
-AHEM-... SO, LET'S BEGIN...
THE SHUFONGFONG ARE GENTLE CREATURES THAT EAT FLOWERS AND PLANTS.
THEY CAN CAMOUFLAGE THEMSELVES TO MATCH THEIR SURROUNDINGS.
COOL!
THEY REALLY ARE BEAUTIFUL!
CLICK
UHH... I CAN'T SEE THEM AT ALL...
SOMEONE TURNED OFF THE LIGHTS!

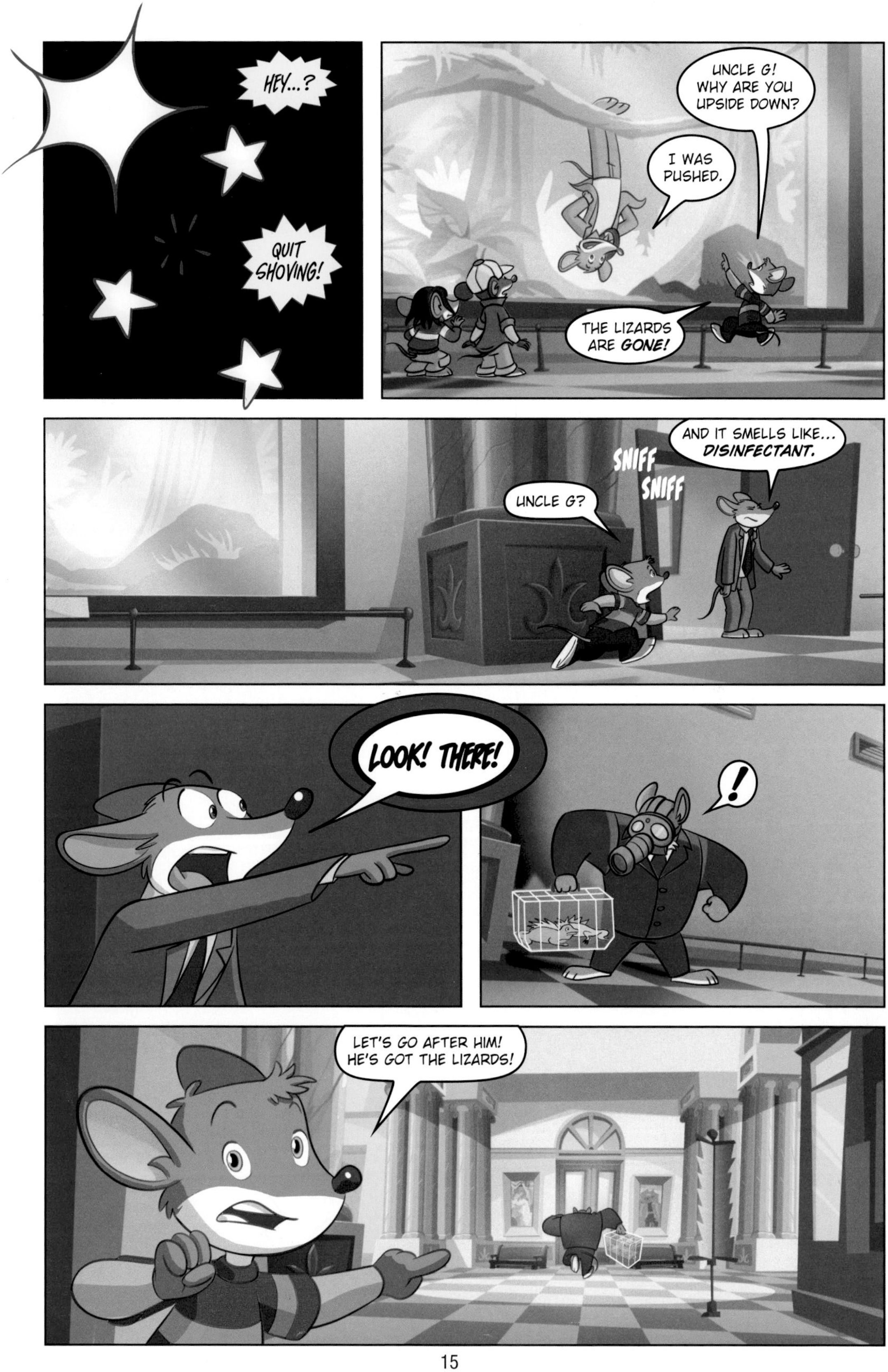
HEY...?
QUIT SHOVING!
UNCLE G! WHY ARE YOU UPSIDE DOWN?
I WAS PUSHED.
THE LIZARDS ARE GONE!
AND IT SMELLS LIKE... DISINFECTANT.
SNIFF SNIFF
UNCLE G?
LOOK! THERE!
!
LET'S GO AFTER HIM! HE'S GOT THE LIZARDS!

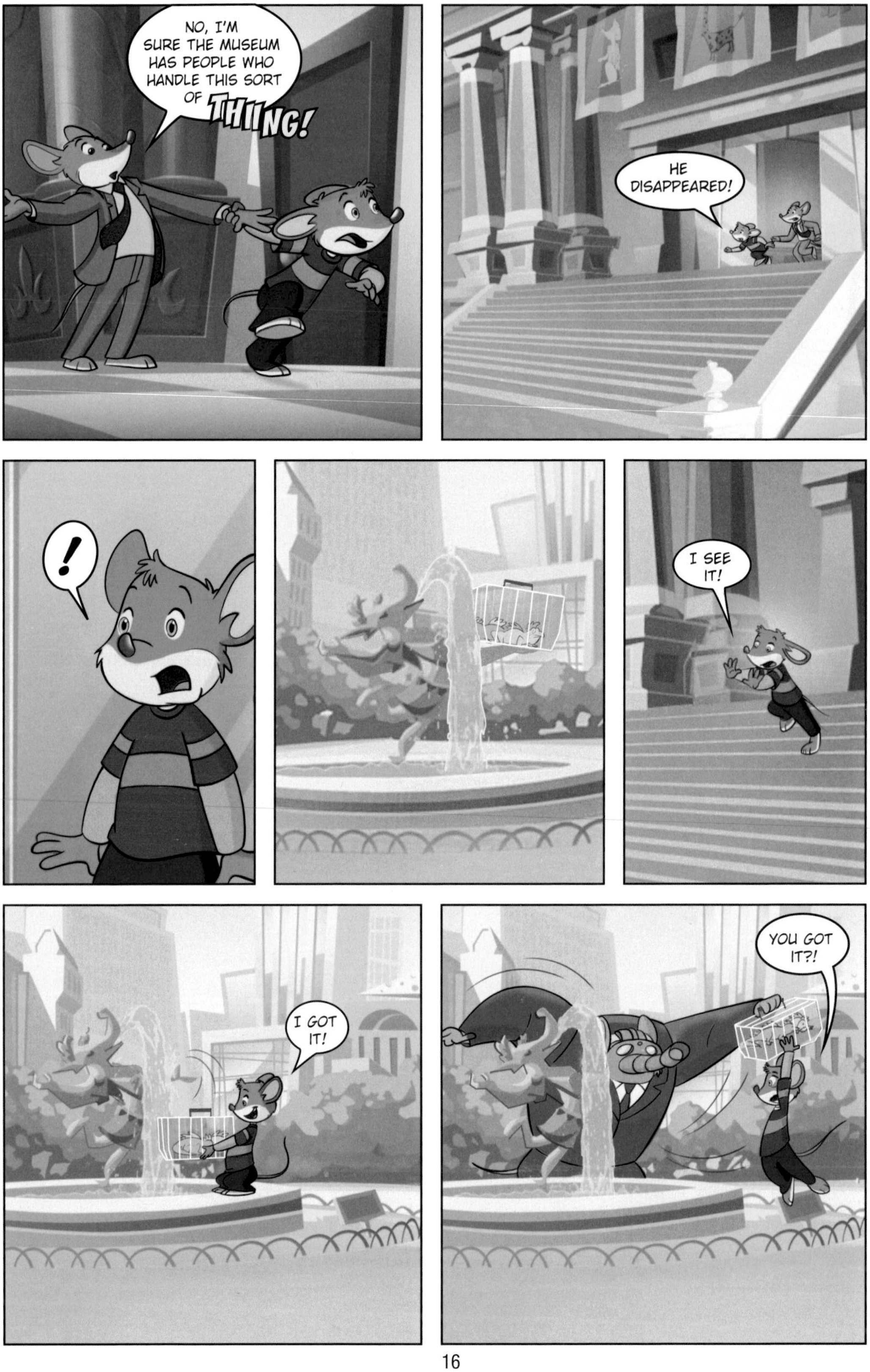
NO, I'M SURE THE MUSEUM HAS PEOPLE WHO HANDLE THIS SORT OF THIIING!
HE DISAPPEARED!
!
I SEE IT!
I GOT IT!
YOU GOT IT?!

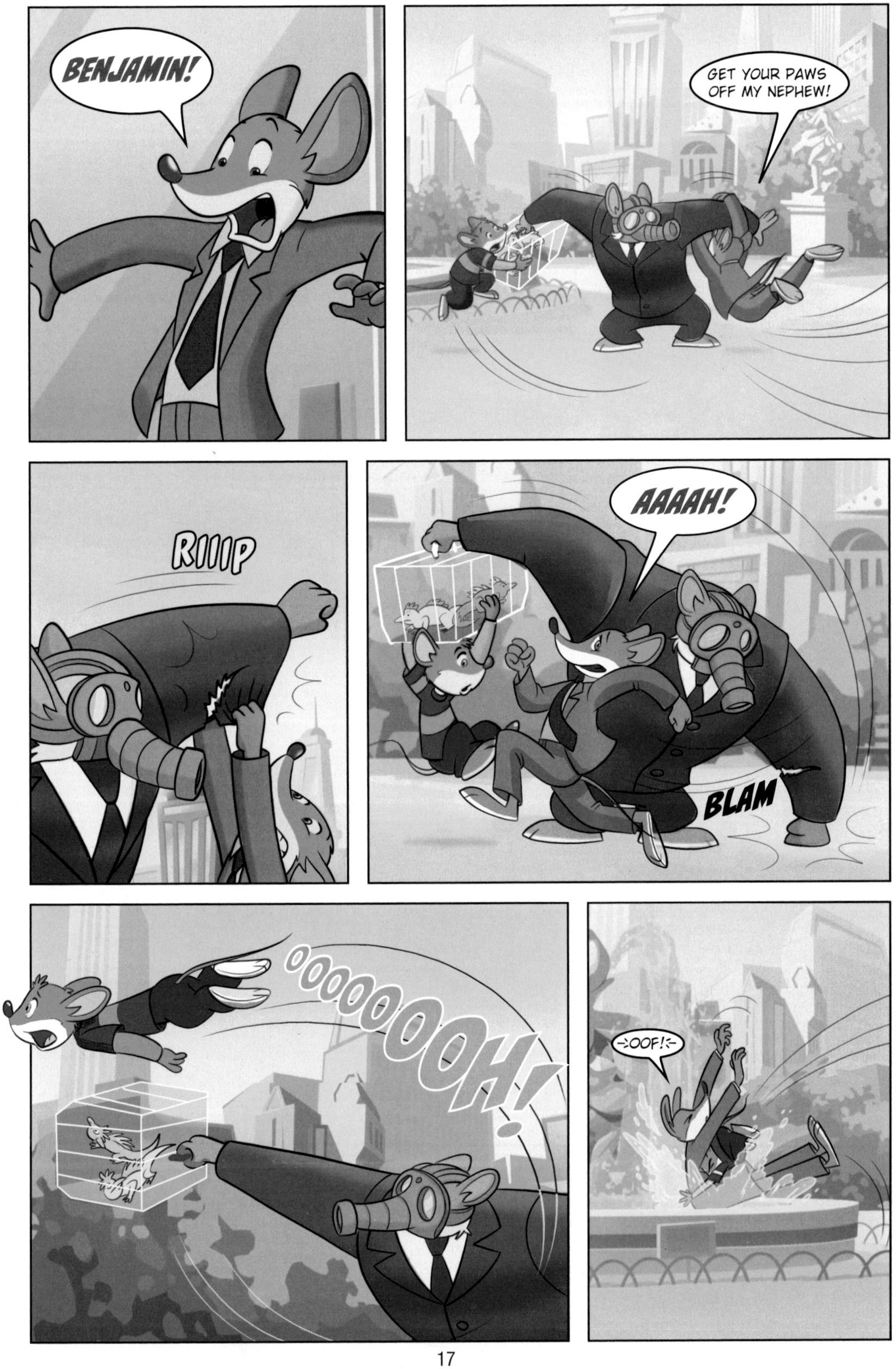

BENJAMIN!
GET YOUR PAWS OFF MY NEPHEW!
RIIIP
AAAAH!
BLAM
OOOOOOOH!
OOF!

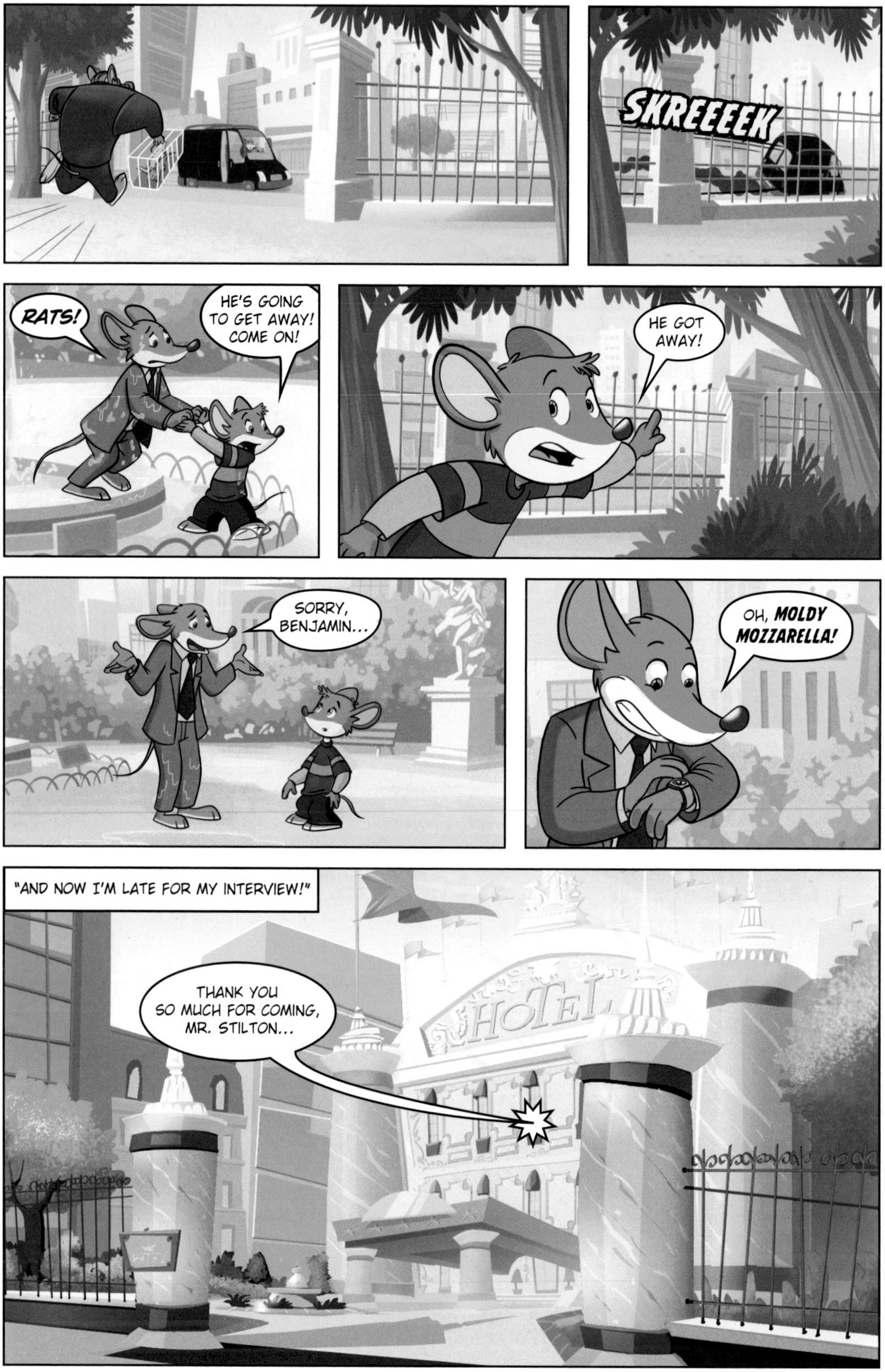

SKREEEEEK
RATS!
HE'S GOING TO GET AWAY! COME ON!
HE GOT AWAY!
SORRY, BENJAMIN...
OH, **MOLDY MOZZARELLA!**
"AND NOW I'M LATE FOR MY INTERVIEW!"
HOTEL
THANK YOU SO MUCH FOR COMING, MR. STILTON...

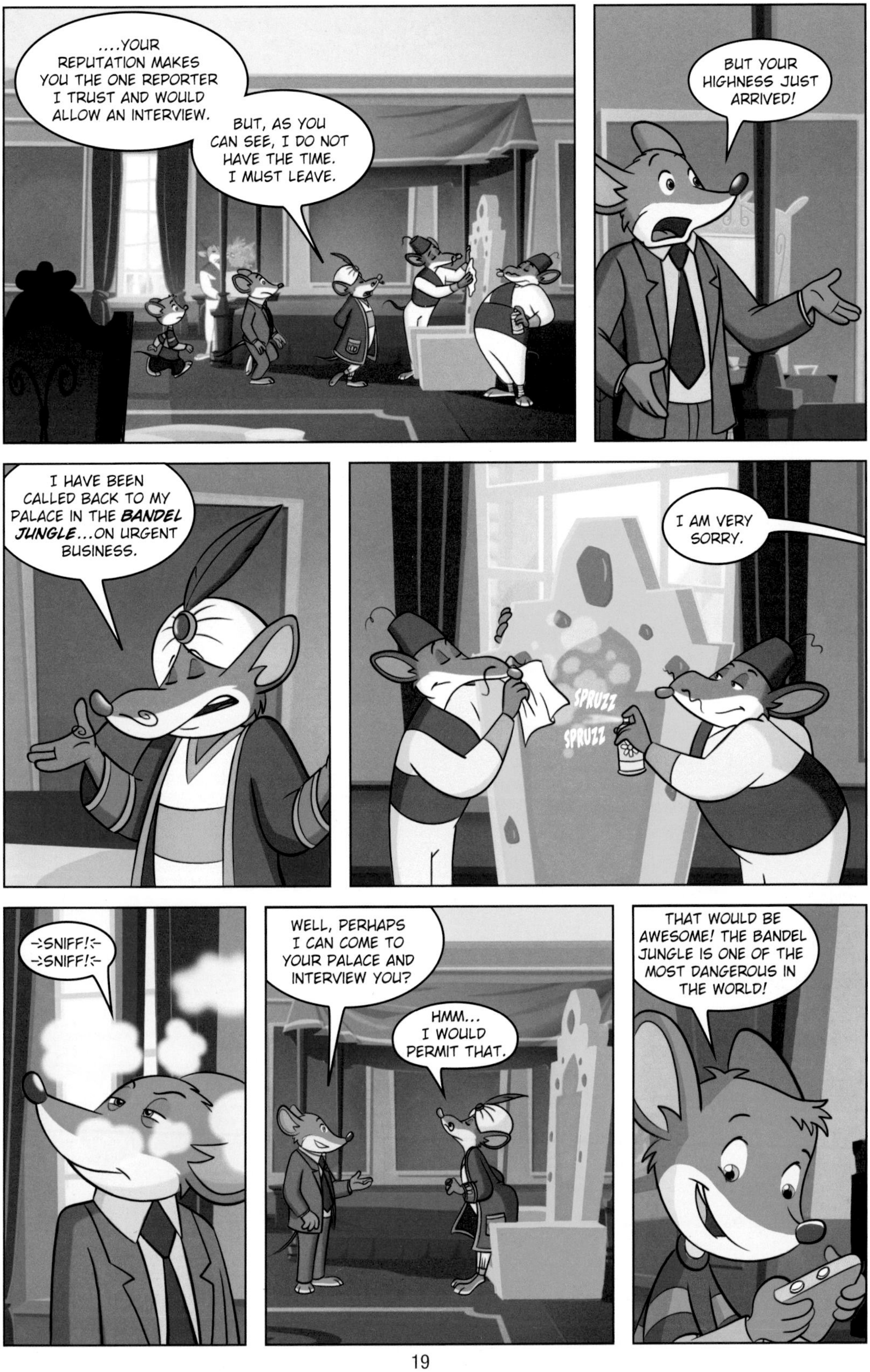
....YOUR REPUTATION MAKES YOU THE ONE REPORTER I TRUST AND WOULD ALLOW AN INTERVIEW.
BUT, AS YOU CAN SEE, I DO NOT HAVE THE TIME. I MUST LEAVE.
BUT YOUR HIGHNESS JUST ARRIVED!
I HAVE BEEN CALLED BACK TO MY PALACE IN THE BANDEL JUNGLE...ON URGENT BUSINESS.
I AM VERY SORRY.
SPRUZZ
SPRUZZ
SNIFF!
SNIFF!
WELL, PERHAPS I CAN COME TO YOUR PALACE AND INTERVIEW YOU?
HMM... I WOULD PERMIT THAT.
THAT WOULD BE AWESOME! THE BANDEL JUNGLE IS ONE OF THE MOST DANGEROUS IN THE WORLD!

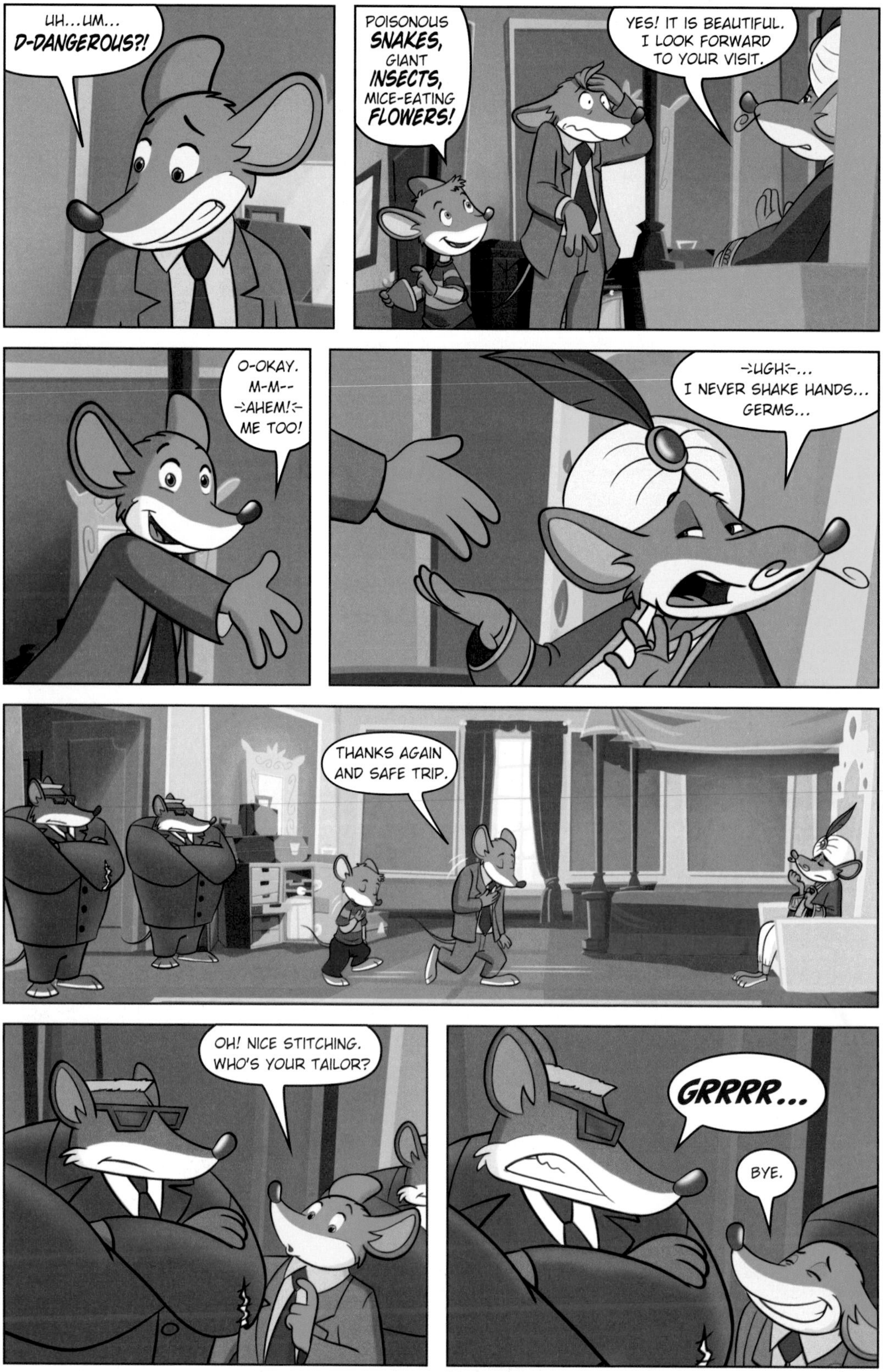

UH...UM... D-DANGEROUS?!
POISONOUS SNAKES, GIANT INSECTS, MICE-EATING FLOWERS!
YES! IT IS BEAUTIFUL. I LOOK FORWARD TO YOUR VISIT.
O-OKAY. M-M-- -AHEM!- ME TOO!
-UGH-... I NEVER SHAKE HANDS... GERMS...
THANKS AGAIN AND SAFE TRIP.
OH! NICE STITCHING. WHO'S YOUR TAILOR?
GRRRR...
BYE.

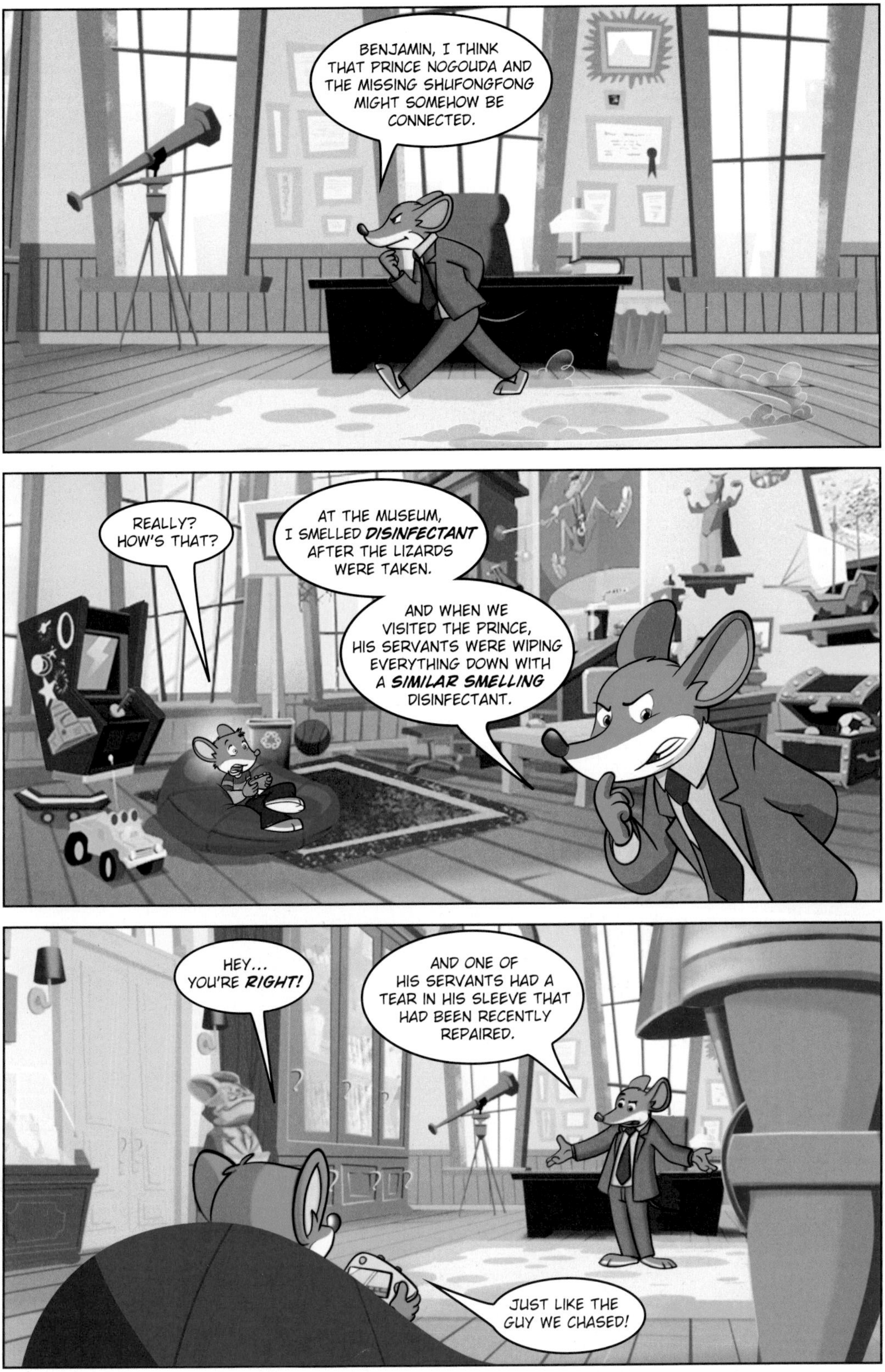
BENJAMIN, I THINK THAT PRINCE NOGOUDA AND THE MISSING SHUFONGFONG MIGHT SOMEHOW BE CONNECTED.
REALLY? HOW'S THAT?
AT THE MUSEUM, I SMELLED **DISINFECTANT** AFTER THE LIZARDS WERE TAKEN.
AND WHEN WE VISITED THE PRINCE, HIS SERVANTS WERE WIPING EVERYTHING DOWN WITH A **SIMILAR SMELLING** DISINFECTANT.
HEY... YOU'RE **RIGHT!**
AND ONE OF HIS SERVANTS HAD A TEAR IN HIS SLEEVE THAT HAD BEEN RECENTLY REPAIRED.
JUST LIKE THE GUY WE CHASED!

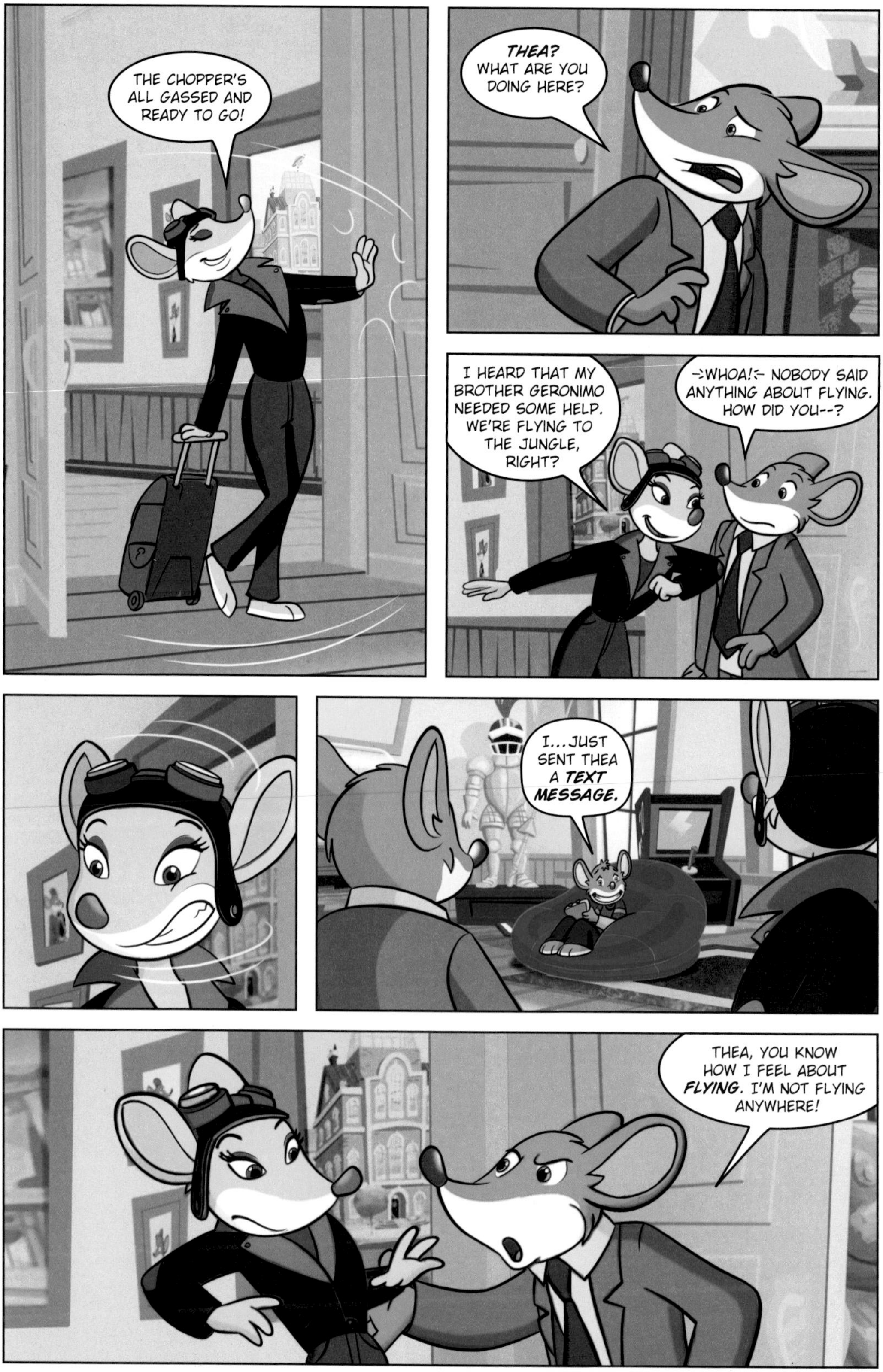
THE CHOPPER'S ALL GASSED AND READY TO GO!
THEA? WHAT ARE YOU DOING HERE?
I HEARD THAT MY BROTHER GERONIMO NEEDED SOME HELP. WE'RE FLYING TO THE JUNGLE, RIGHT?
WHOA! NOBODY SAID ANYTHING ABOUT FLYING. HOW DID YOU--?
I...JUST SENT THEA A *TEXT MESSAGE.*
THEA, YOU KNOW HOW I FEEL ABOUT *FLYING*. I'M NOT FLYING ANYWHERE!

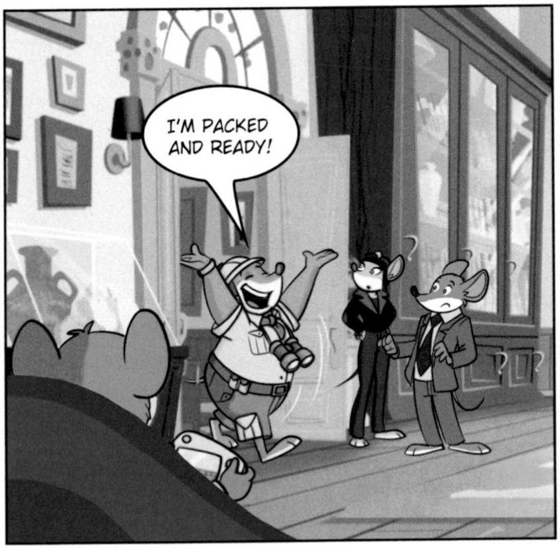
I'M PACKED AND READY!

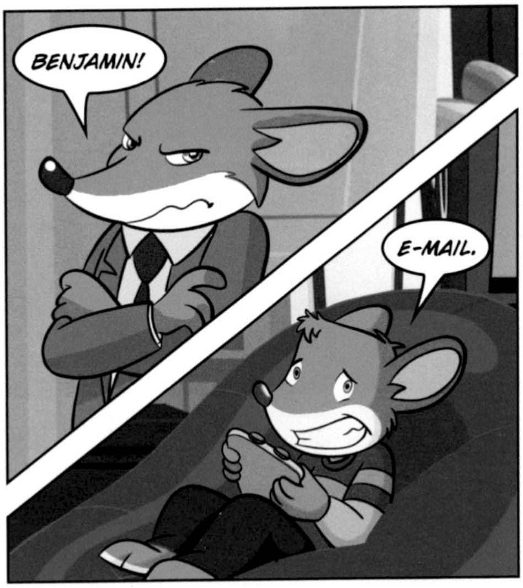
BENJAMIN!
E-MAIL.

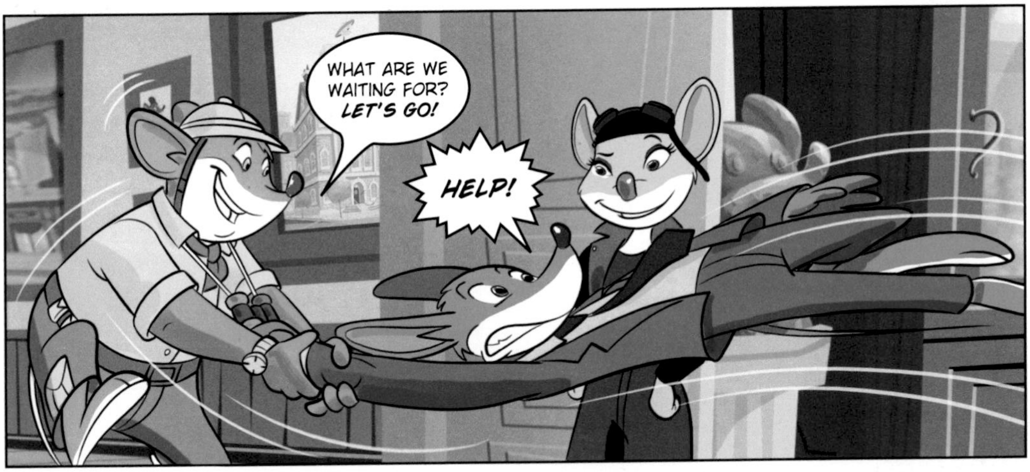
WHAT ARE WE WAITING FOR? LET'S GO!
HELP!

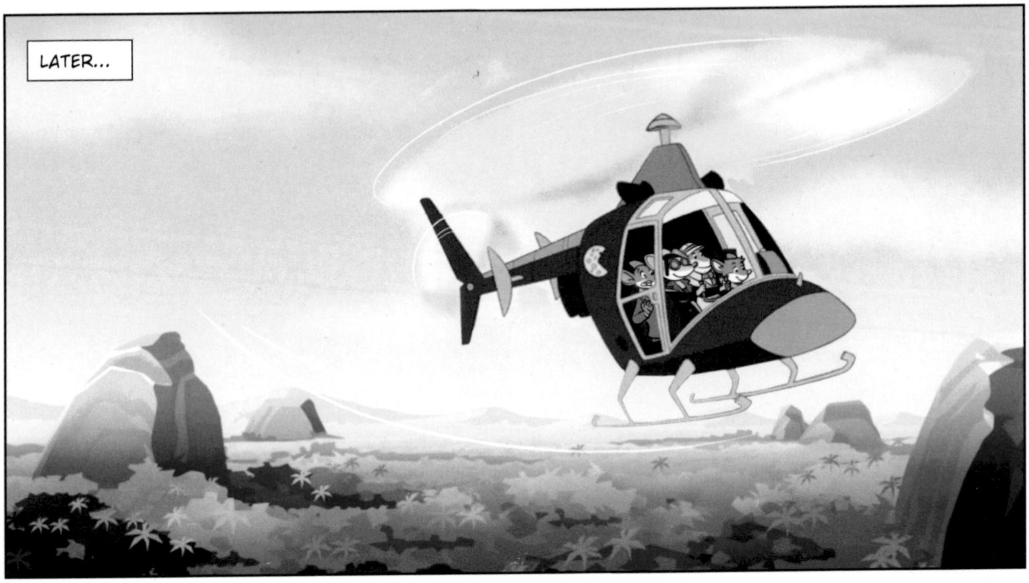
LATER...

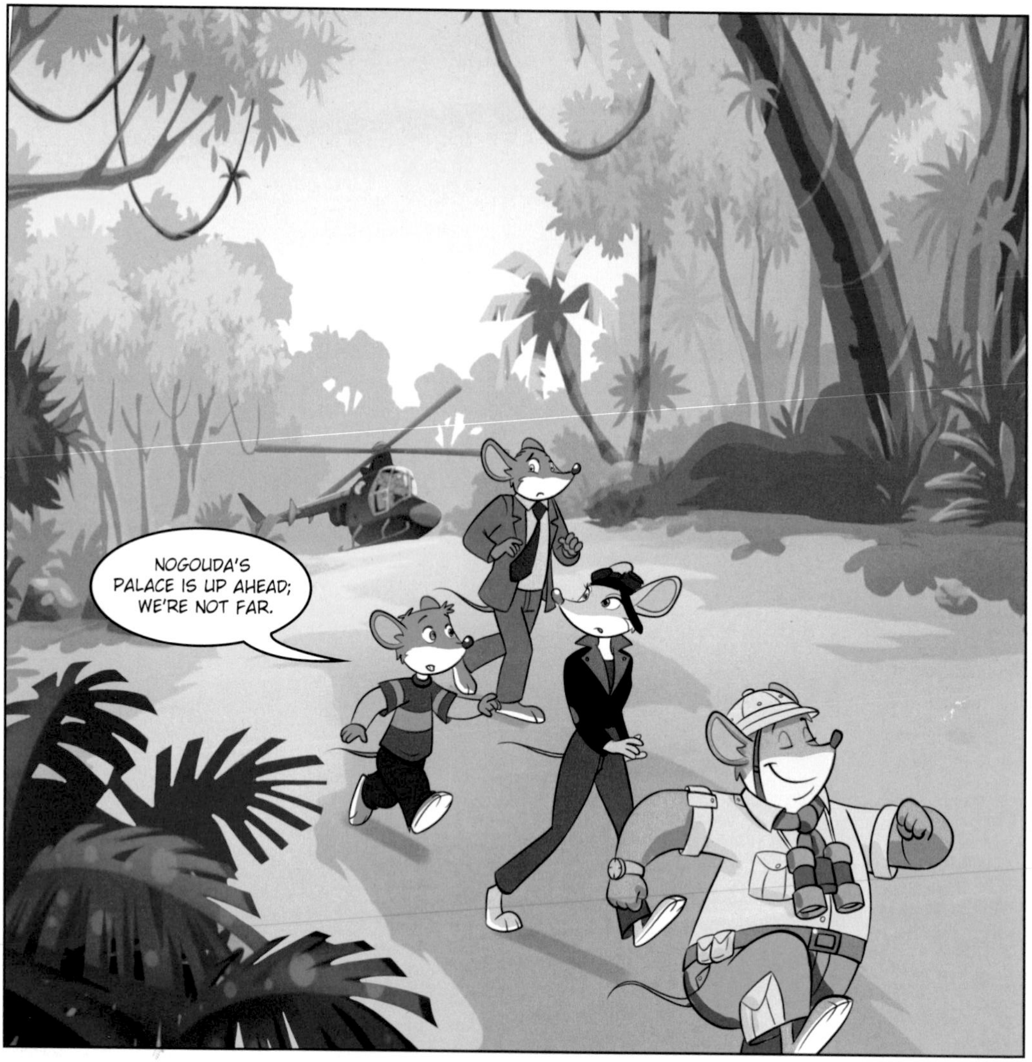
NOGOUDA'S PALACE IS UP AHEAD; WE'RE NOT FAR.

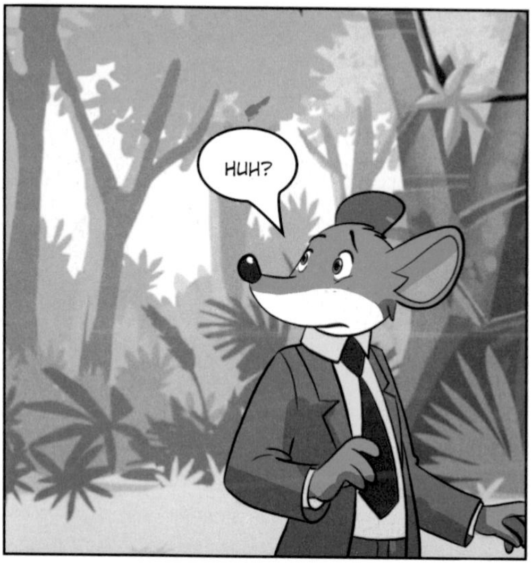
HUH?

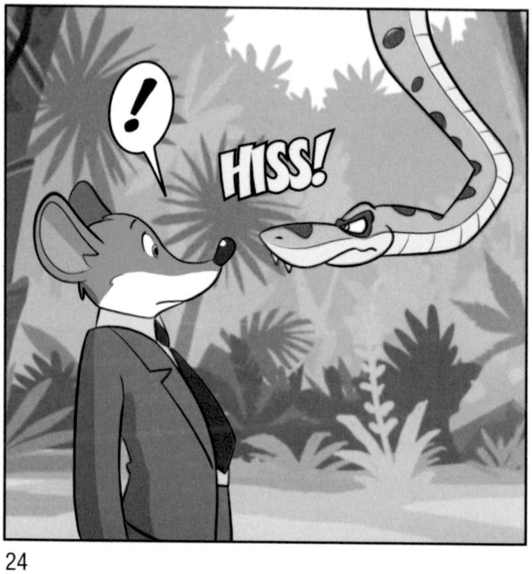
!
HISS!

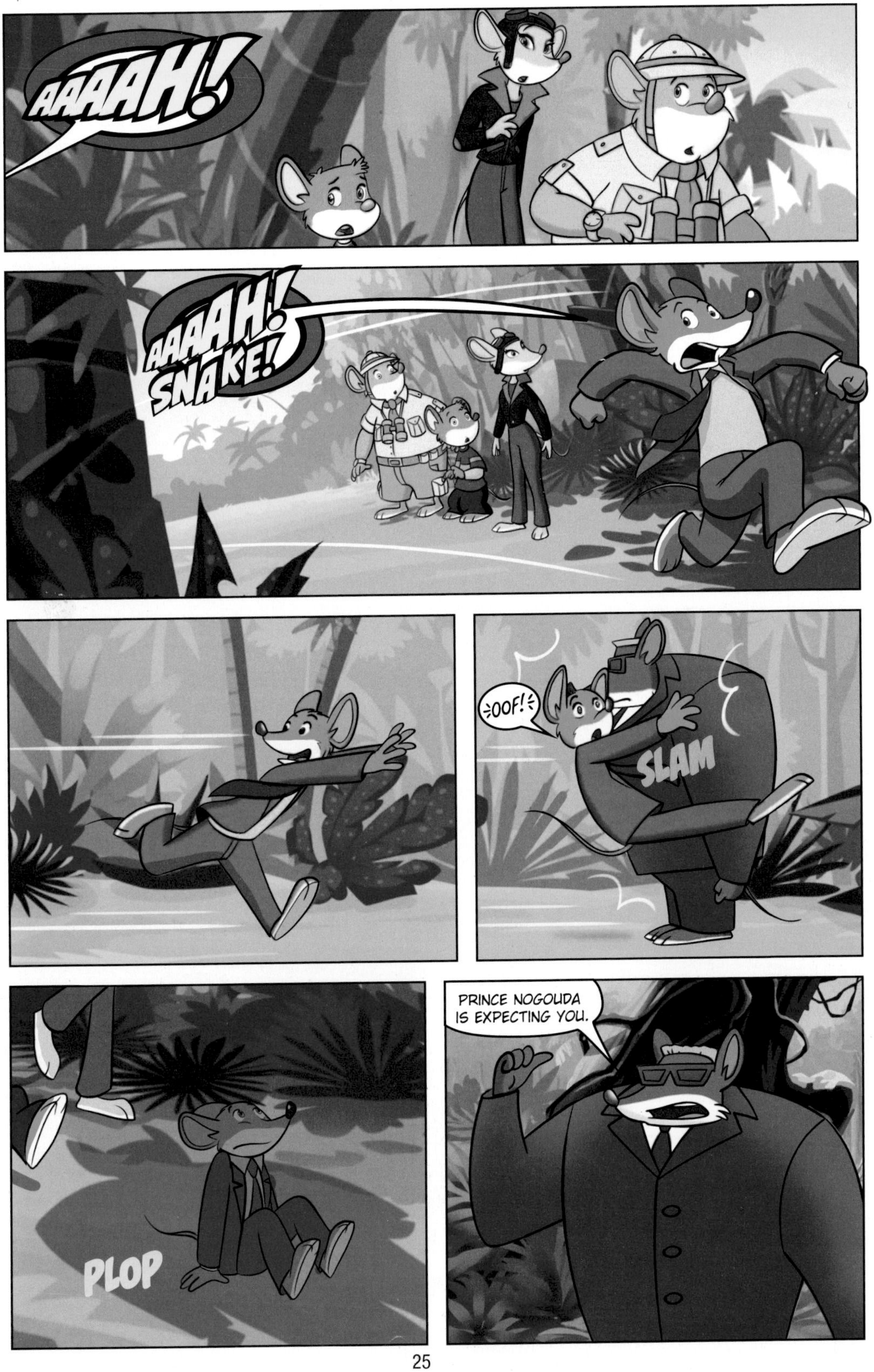
AAAAH!
AAAAH! SNAKE!
OOF!
SLAM
PLOP
PRINCE NOGOUDA IS EXPECTING YOU.

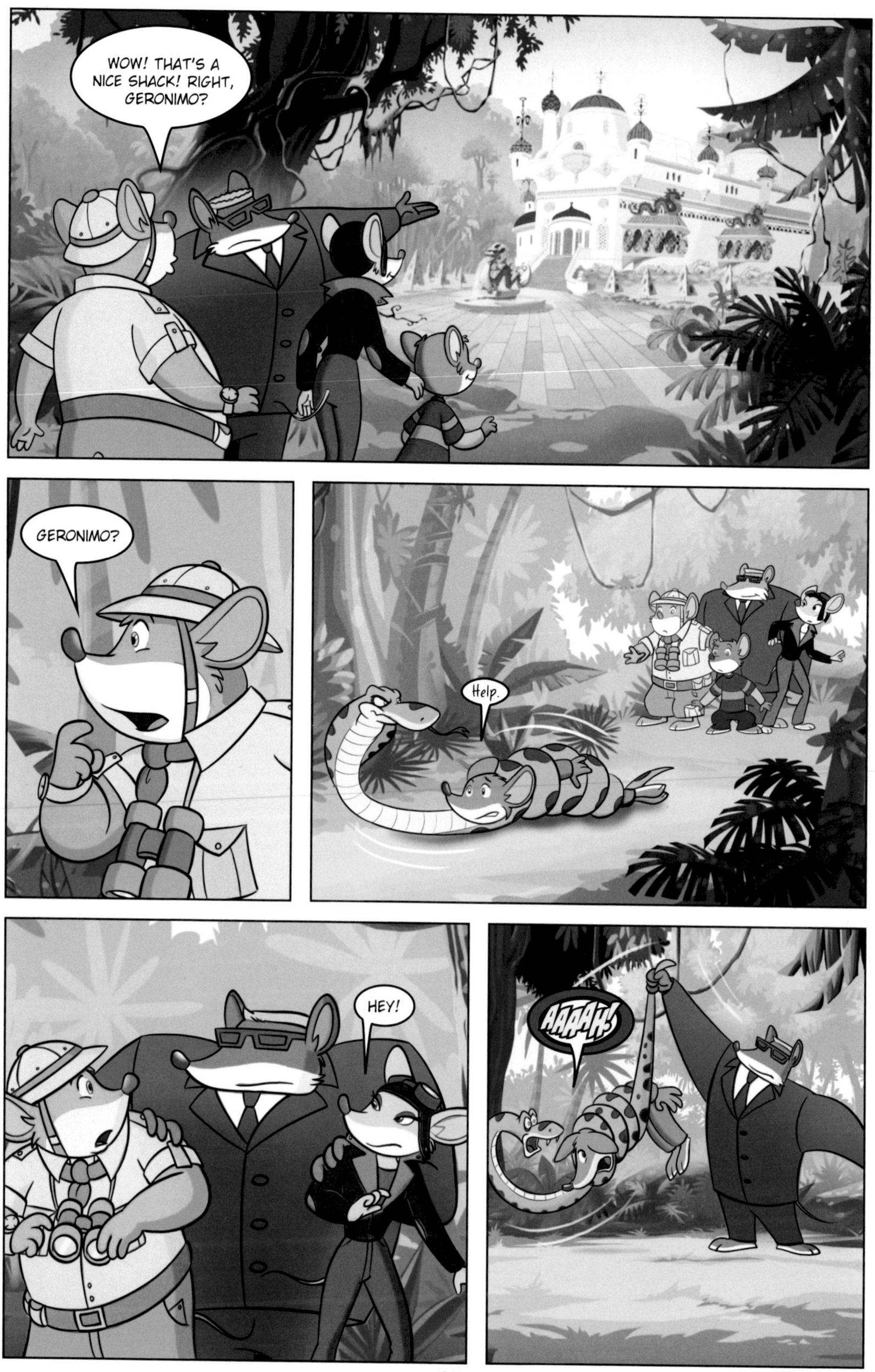
WOW! THAT'S A NICE SHACK! RIGHT, GERONIMO?
GERONIMO?
Help.
HEY!
AAAAH!

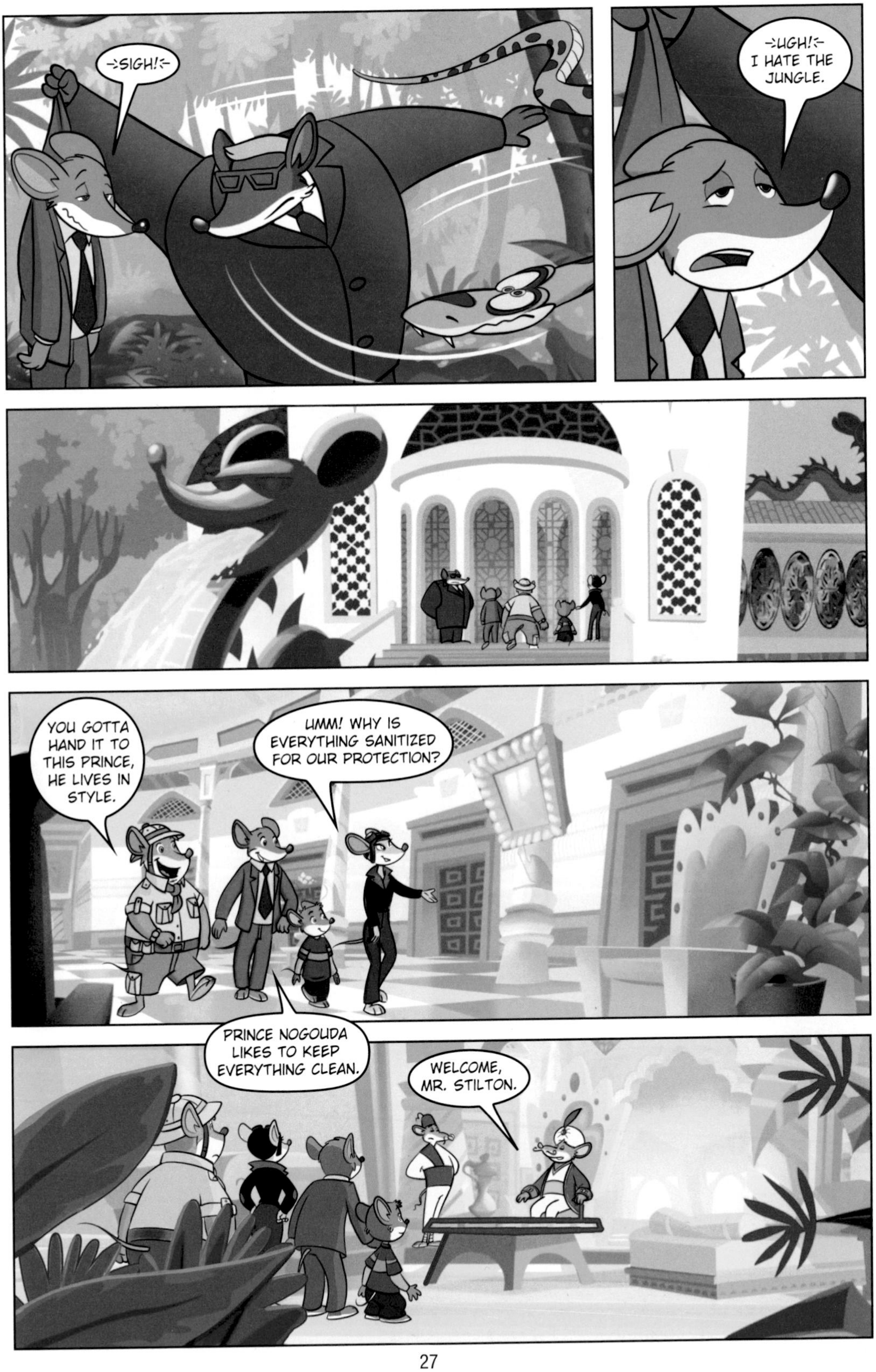
SIGH!
UGH! I HATE THE JUNGLE.
YOU GOTTA HAND IT TO THIS PRINCE, HE LIVES IN STYLE.
UMM! WHY IS EVERYTHING SANITIZED FOR OUR PROTECTION?
PRINCE NOGOUDA LIKES TO KEEP EVERYTHING CLEAN.
WELCOME, MR. STILTON.

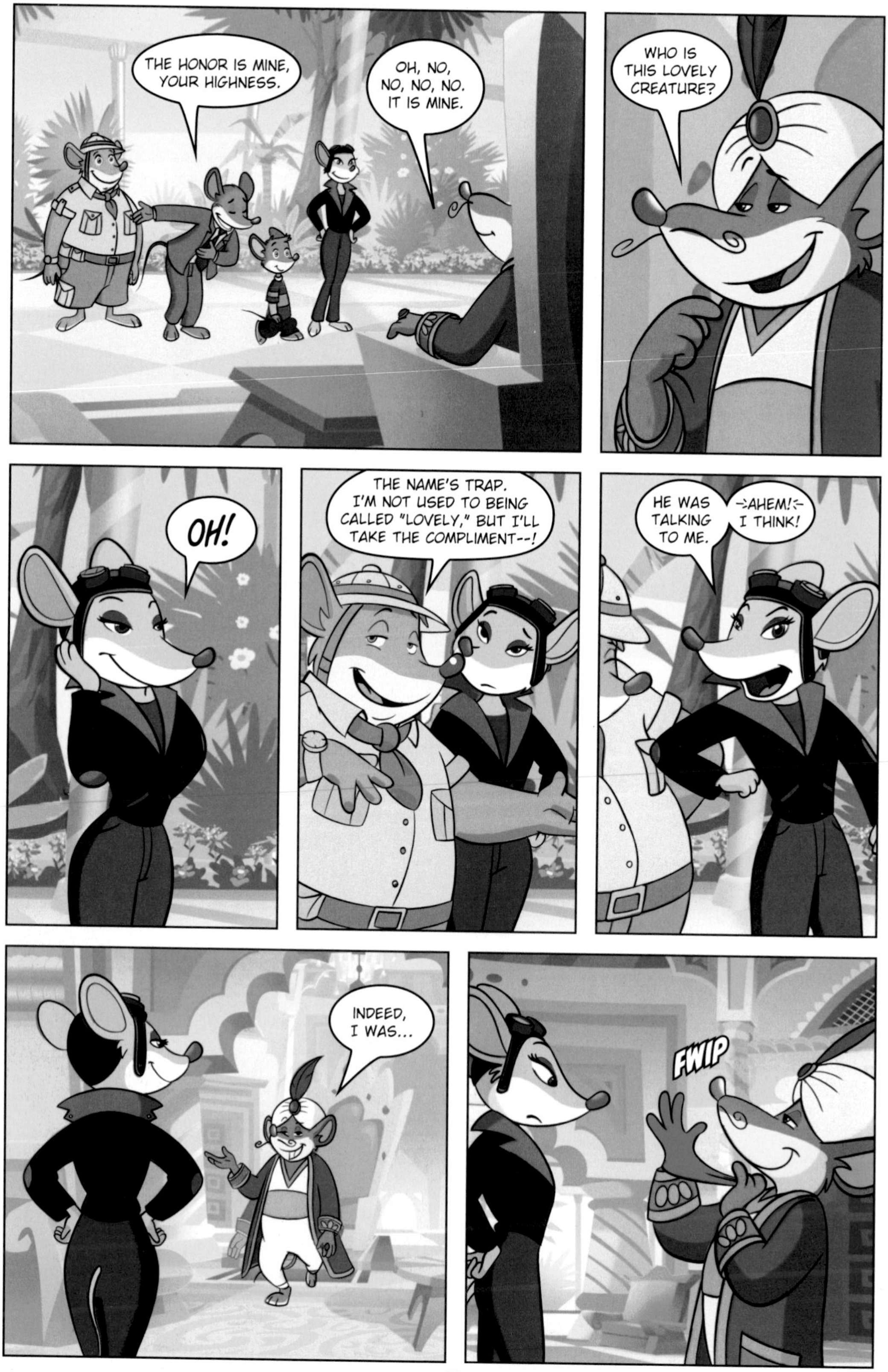
THE HONOR IS MINE, YOUR HIGHNESS.
OH, NO, NO, NO, NO. IT IS MINE.
WHO IS THIS LOVELY CREATURE?
OH!
THE NAME'S TRAP. I'M NOT USED TO BEING CALLED "LOVELY," BUT I'LL TAKE THE COMPLIMENT--!
HE WAS TALKING TO ME.
AHEM! I THINK!
INDEED, I WAS...
FWIP

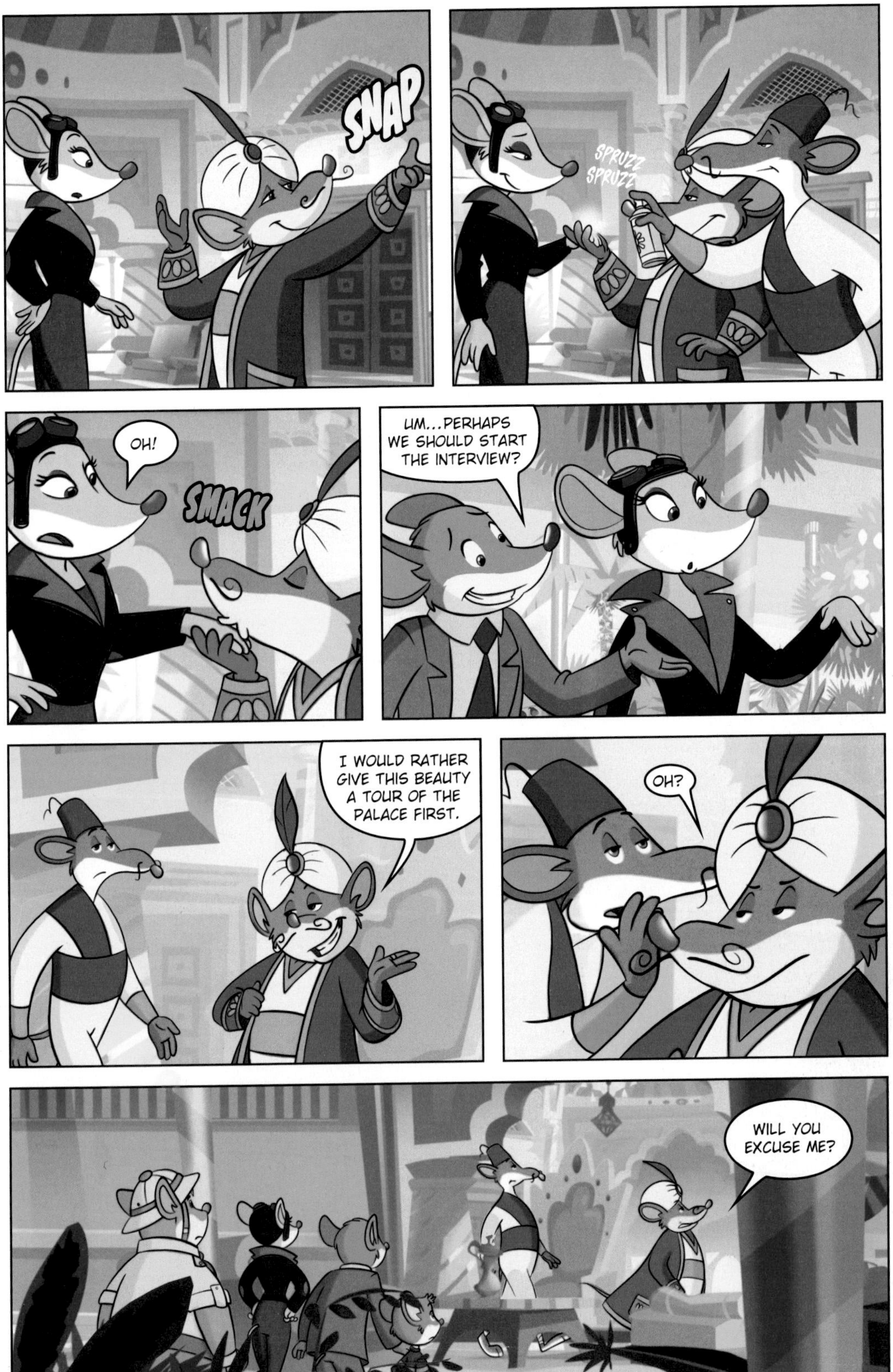
SNAP
SPRUZZ SPRUZZ
OH!
SMACK
UM...PERHAPS WE SHOULD START THE INTERVIEW?
I WOULD RATHER GIVE THIS BEAUTY A TOUR OF THE PALACE FIRST.
OH?
WILL YOU EXCUSE ME?

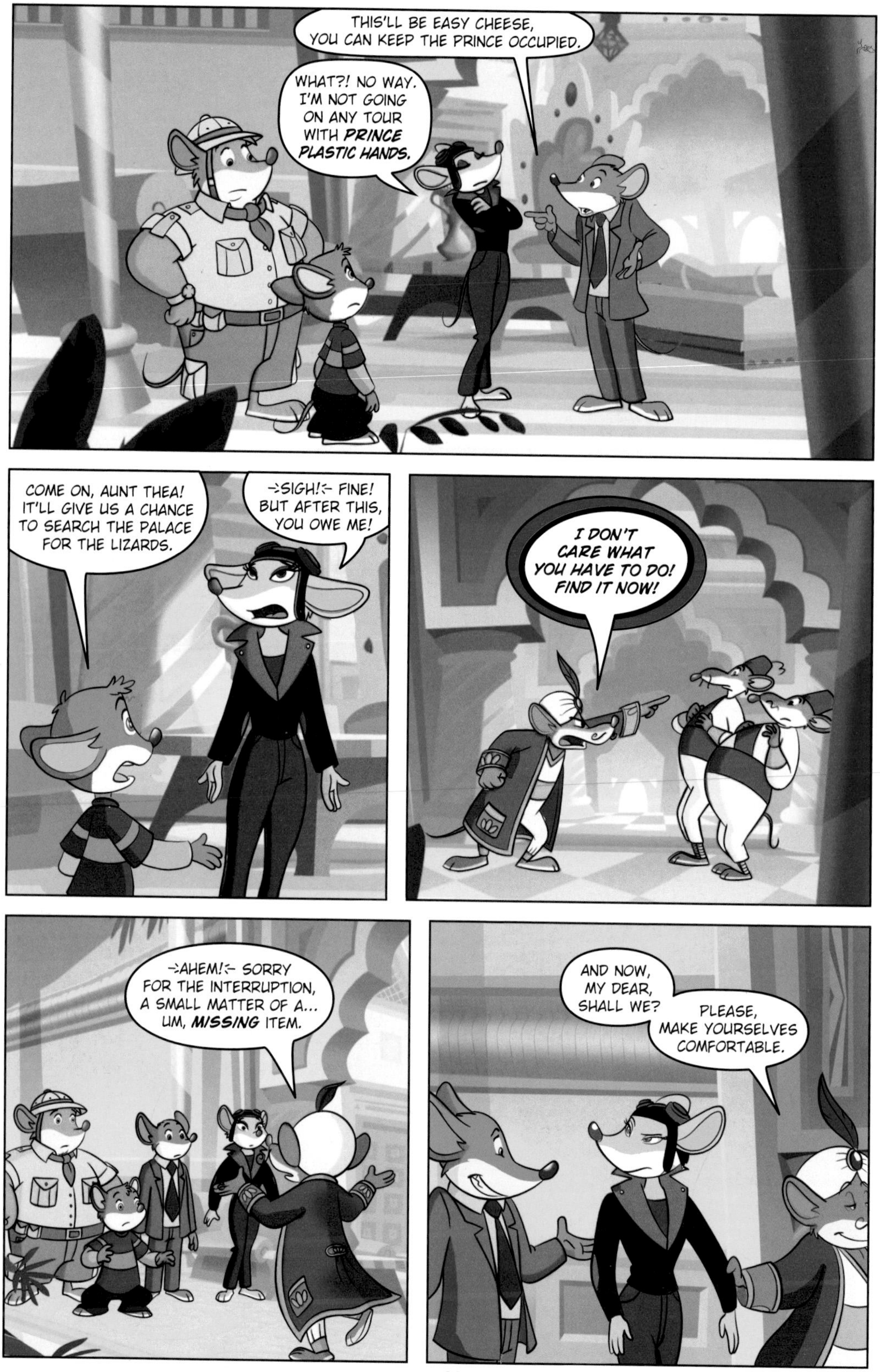
THIS'LL BE EASY CHEESE, YOU CAN KEEP THE PRINCE OCCUPIED.
WHAT?! NO WAY. I'M NOT GOING ON ANY TOUR WITH **PRINCE PLASTIC HANDS.**
COME ON, AUNT THEA! IT'LL GIVE US A CHANCE TO SEARCH THE PALACE FOR THE LIZARDS.
-SIGH!- FINE! BUT AFTER THIS, YOU OWE ME!
I DON'T CARE WHAT YOU HAVE TO DO! FIND IT NOW!
-AHEM!- SORRY FOR THE INTERRUPTION, A SMALL MATTER OF A... UM, **MISSING** ITEM.
AND NOW, MY DEAR, SHALL WE?
PLEASE, MAKE YOURSELVES COMFORTABLE.

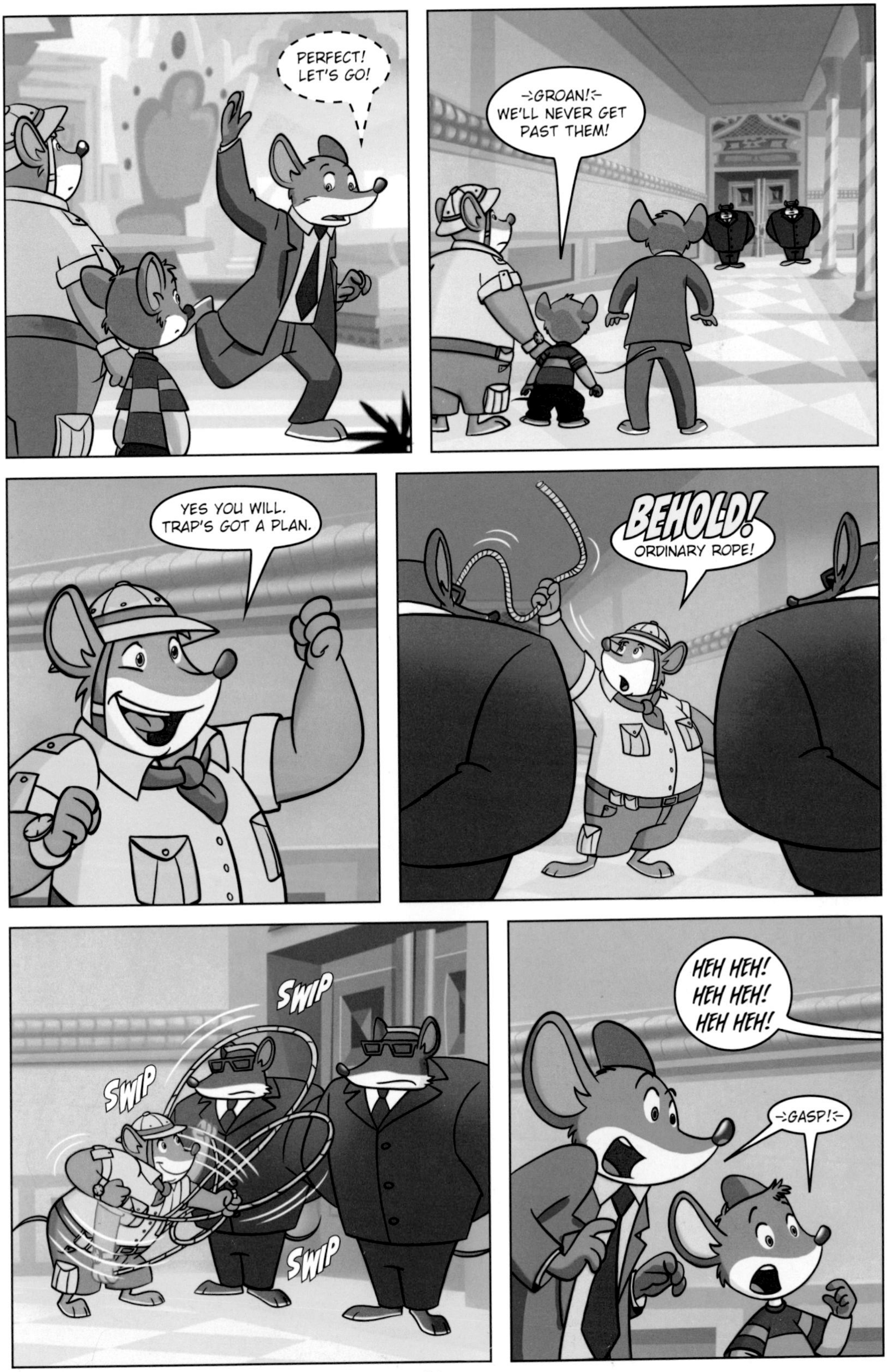
PERFECT! LET'S GO!
-GROAN!- WE'LL NEVER GET PAST THEM!
YES YOU WILL. TRAP'S GOT A PLAN.
BEHOLD! ORDINARY ROPE!
SWIP
SWIP
SWIP
HEH HEH! HEH HEH! HEH HEH!
-GASP!-

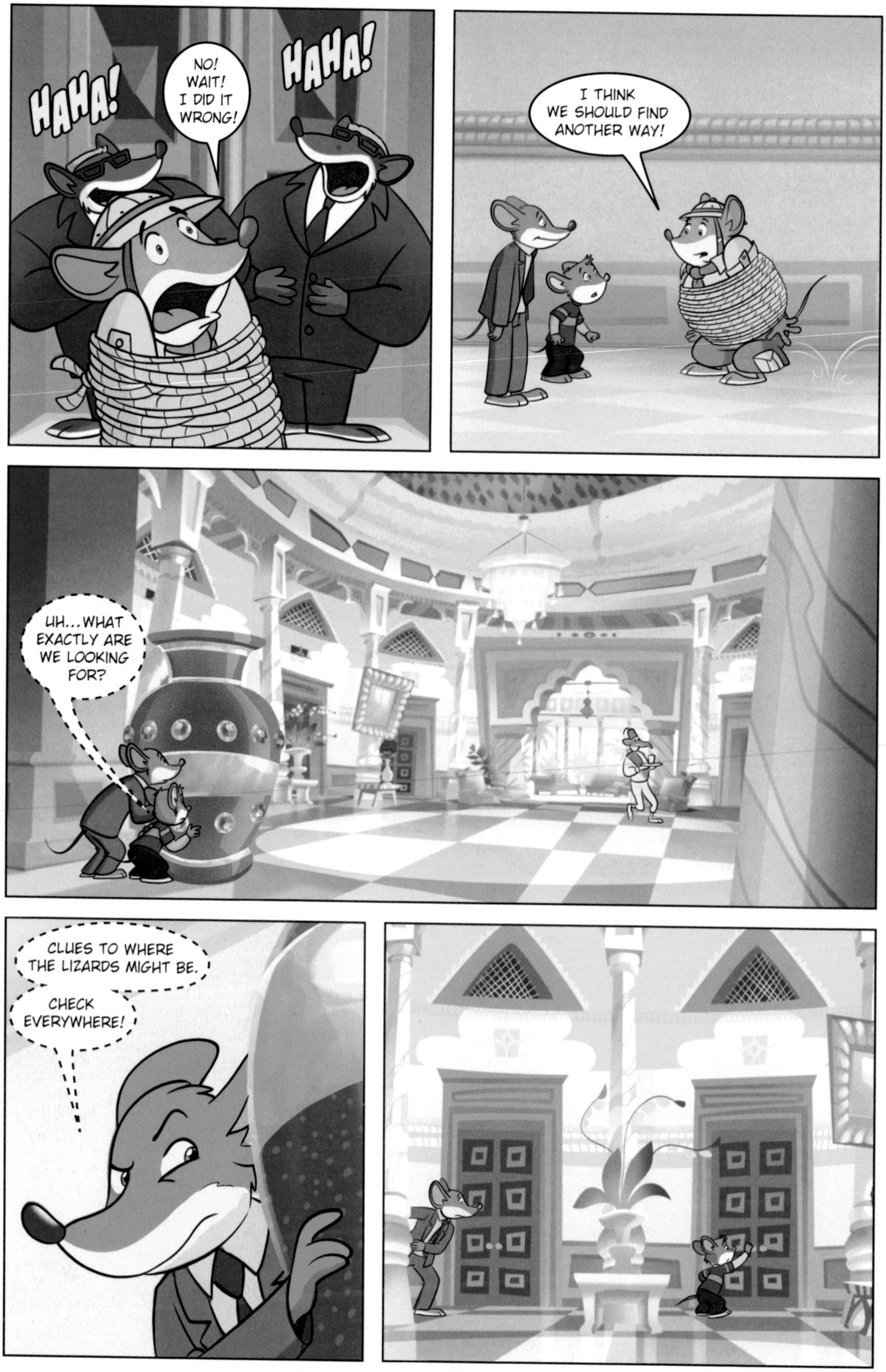
HAHA!
NO! WAIT! I DID IT WRONG!
HAHA!
I THINK WE SHOULD FIND ANOTHER WAY!
UH...WHAT EXACTLY ARE WE LOOKING FOR?
CLUES TO WHERE THE LIZARDS MIGHT BE.
CHECK EVERYWHERE!

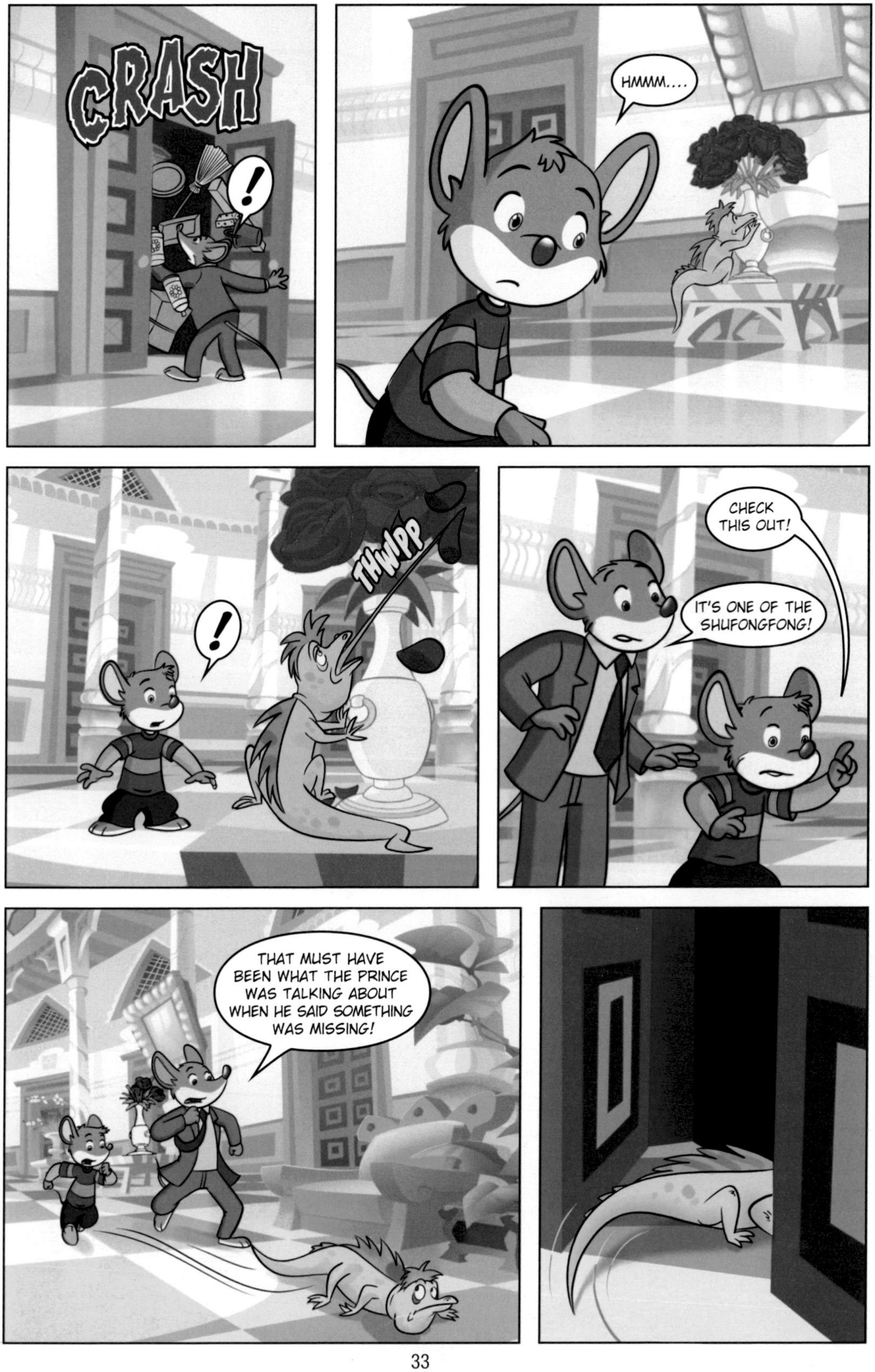
CRASH
!
HMMM....
THWIPP
!
CHECK THIS OUT!
IT'S ONE OF THE SHUFONGFONG!
THAT MUST HAVE BEEN WHAT THE PRINCE WAS TALKING ABOUT WHEN HE SAID SOMETHING WAS MISSING!

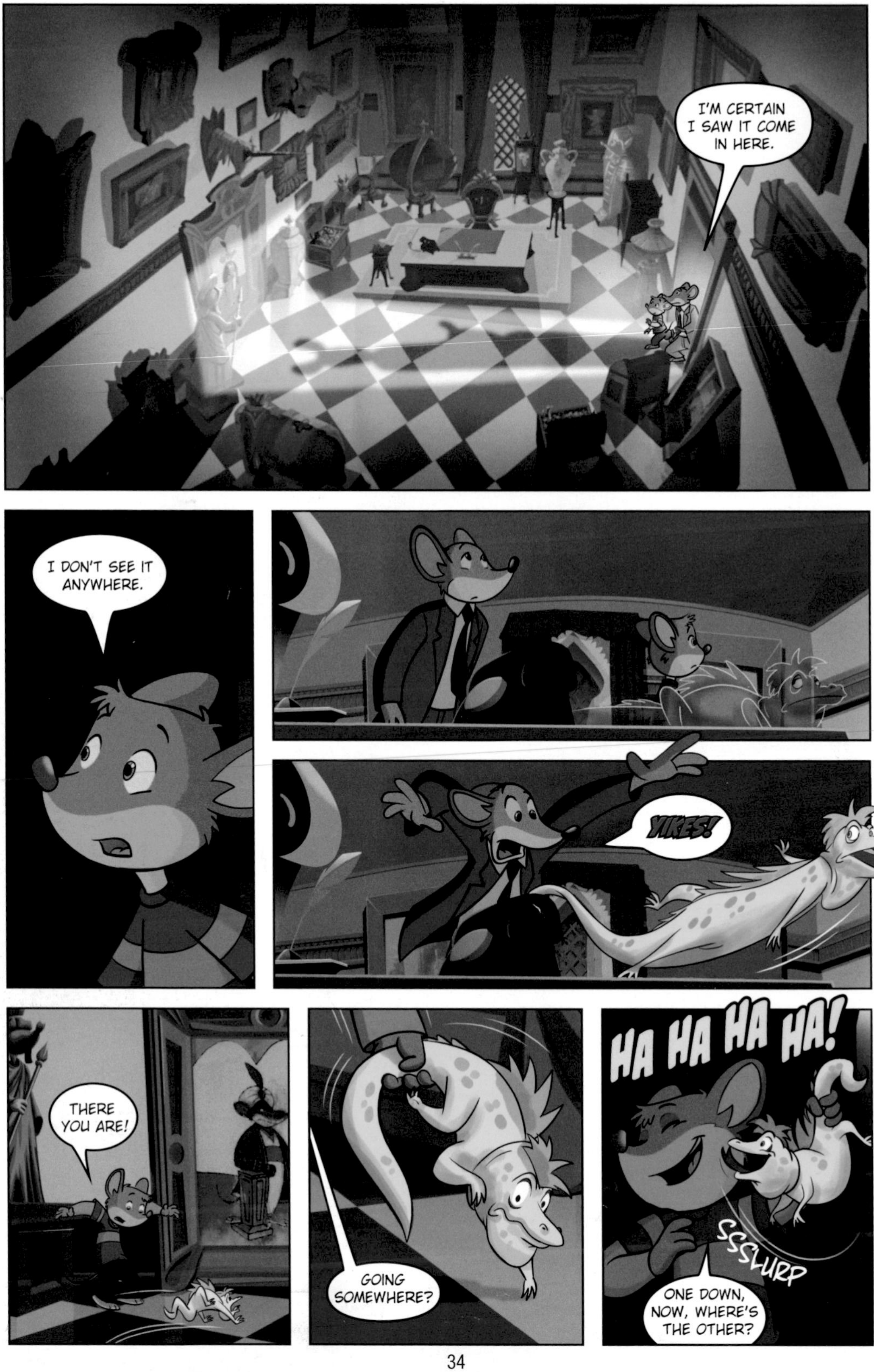

I'M CERTAIN I SAW IT COME IN HERE.
I DON'T SEE IT ANYWHERE.
YIKES!
THERE YOU ARE!
GOING SOMEWHERE?
HA HA HA HA!
SSSLURP
ONE DOWN, NOW, WHERE'S THE OTHER?

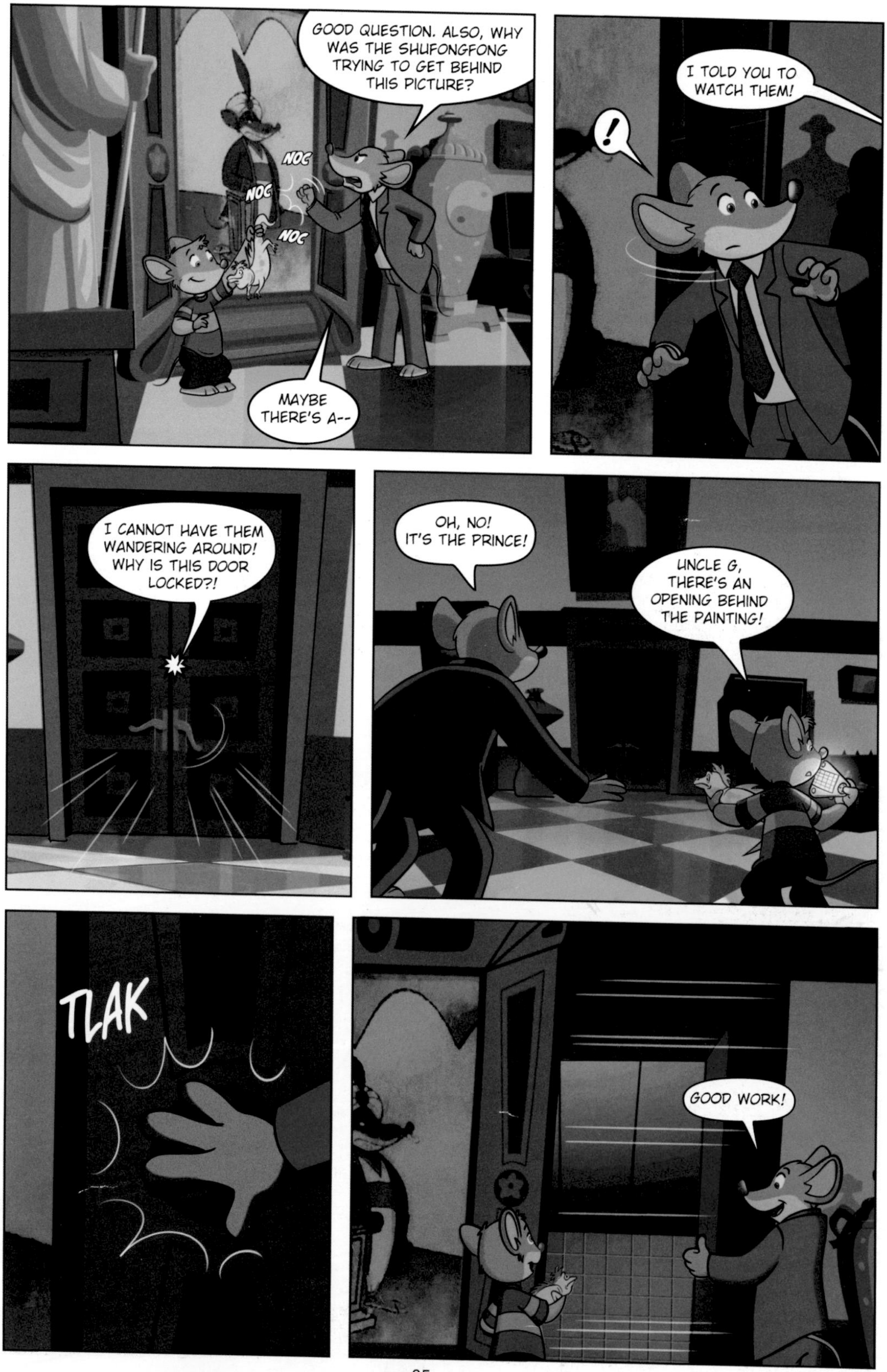
GOOD QUESTION. ALSO, WHY WAS THE SHUFONGFONG TRYING TO GET BEHIND THIS PICTURE?
NOC
NOC
NOC
MAYBE THERE'S A--
I TOLD YOU TO WATCH THEM!
!
I CANNOT HAVE THEM WANDERING AROUND! WHY IS THIS DOOR LOCKED?!
OH, NO! IT'S THE PRINCE!
UNCLE G, THERE'S AN OPENING BEHIND THE PAINTING!
TLAK
GOOD WORK!

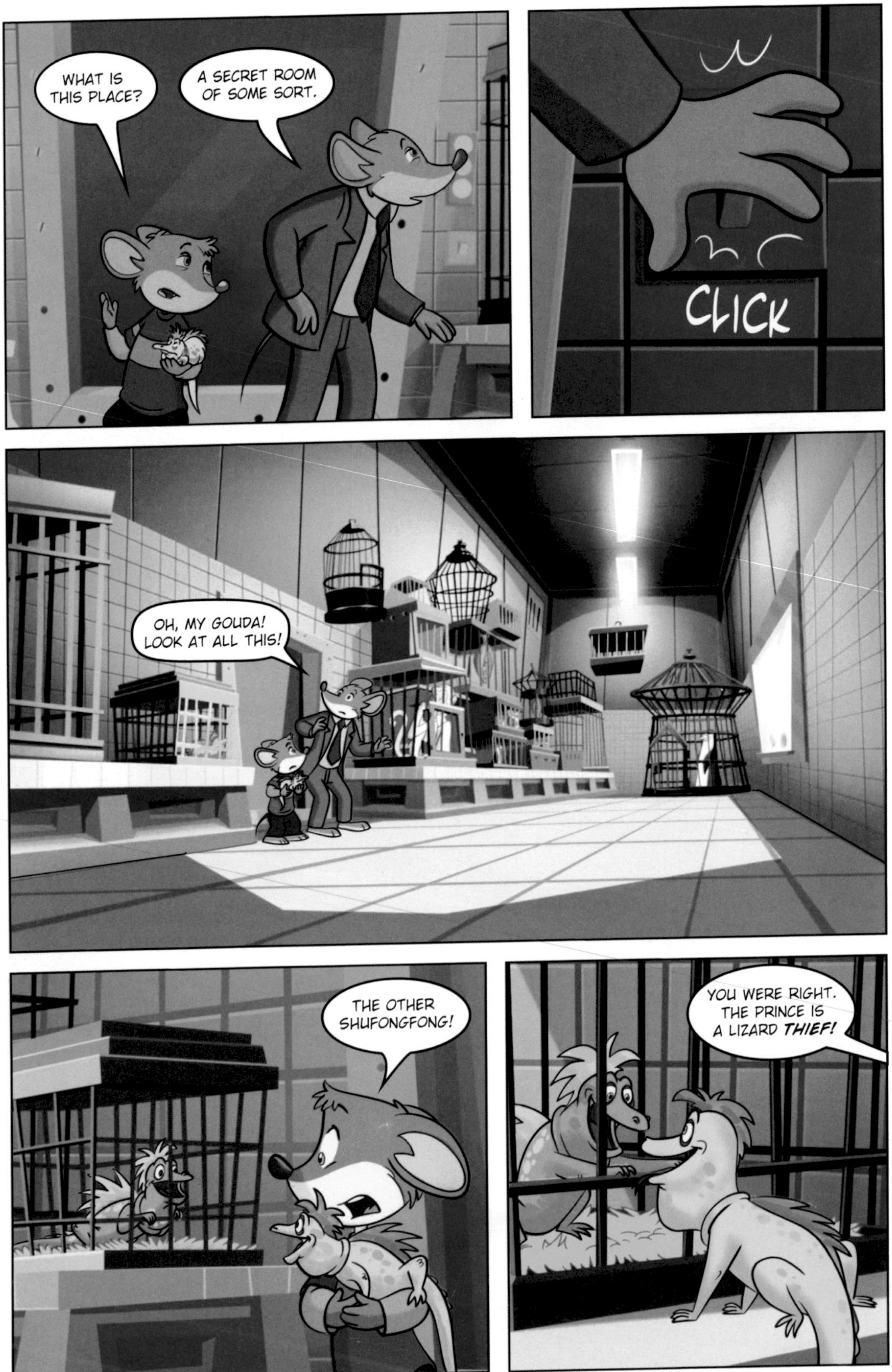
WHAT IS THIS PLACE?
A SECRET ROOM OF SOME SORT.
CLICK
OH, MY GOUDA! LOOK AT ALL THIS!
THE OTHER SHUFONGFONG!
YOU WERE RIGHT. THE PRINCE IS A LIZARD *THIEF!*

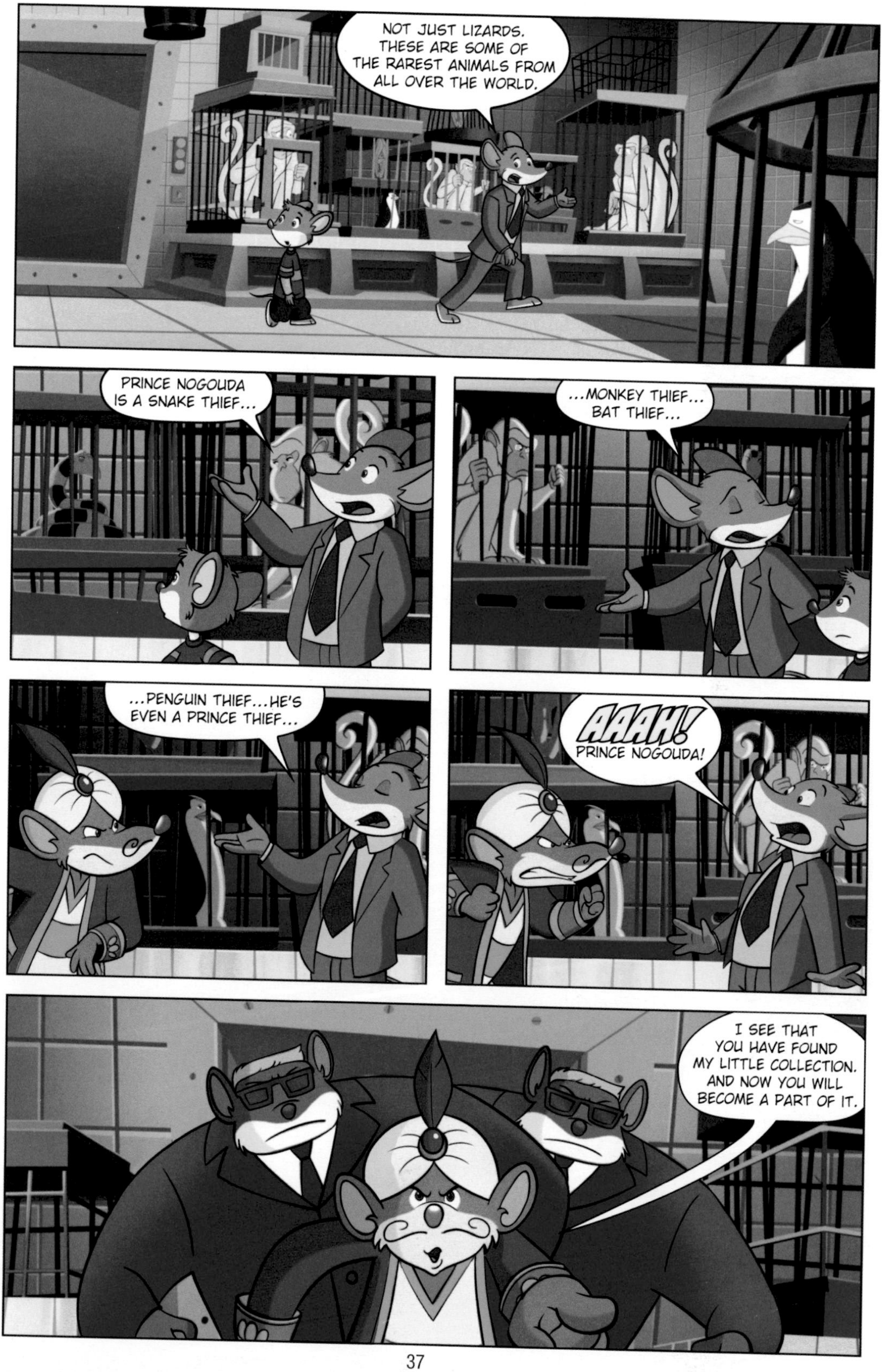
NOT JUST LIZARDS. THESE ARE SOME OF THE RAREST ANIMALS FROM ALL OVER THE WORLD.
PRINCE NOGOUDA IS A SNAKE THIEF...
...MONKEY THIEF... BAT THIEF...
...PENGUIN THIEF...HE'S EVEN A PRINCE THIEF...
AAAH! PRINCE NOGOUDA!
I SEE THAT YOU HAVE FOUND MY LITTLE COLLECTION. AND NOW YOU WILL BECOME A PART OF IT.

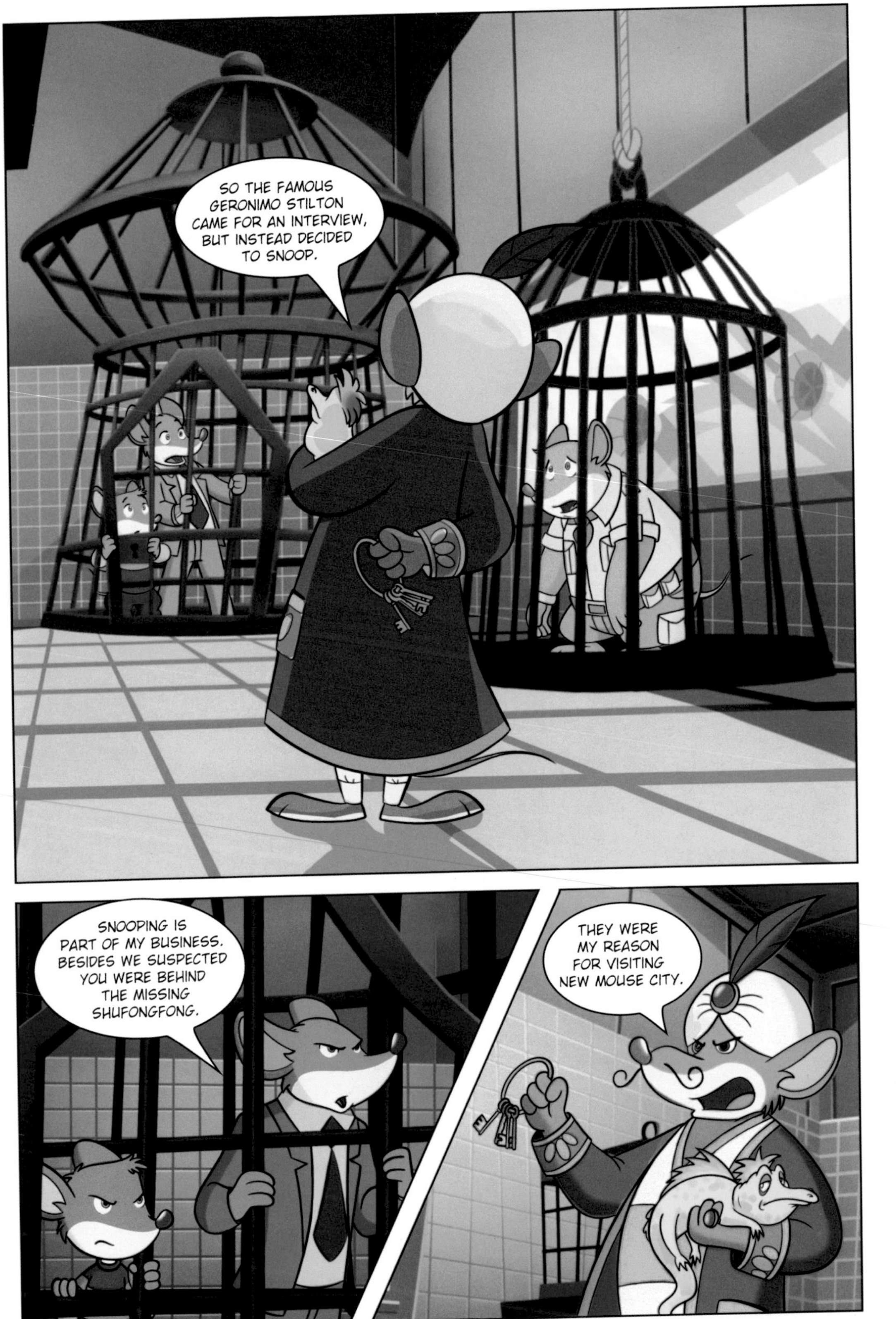
SO THE FAMOUS GERONIMO STILTON CAME FOR AN INTERVIEW, BUT INSTEAD DECIDED TO SNOOP.
SNOOPING IS PART OF MY BUSINESS. BESIDES WE SUSPECTED YOU WERE BEHIND THE MISSING SHUFONGFONG.
THEY WERE MY REASON FOR VISITING NEW MOUSE CITY.

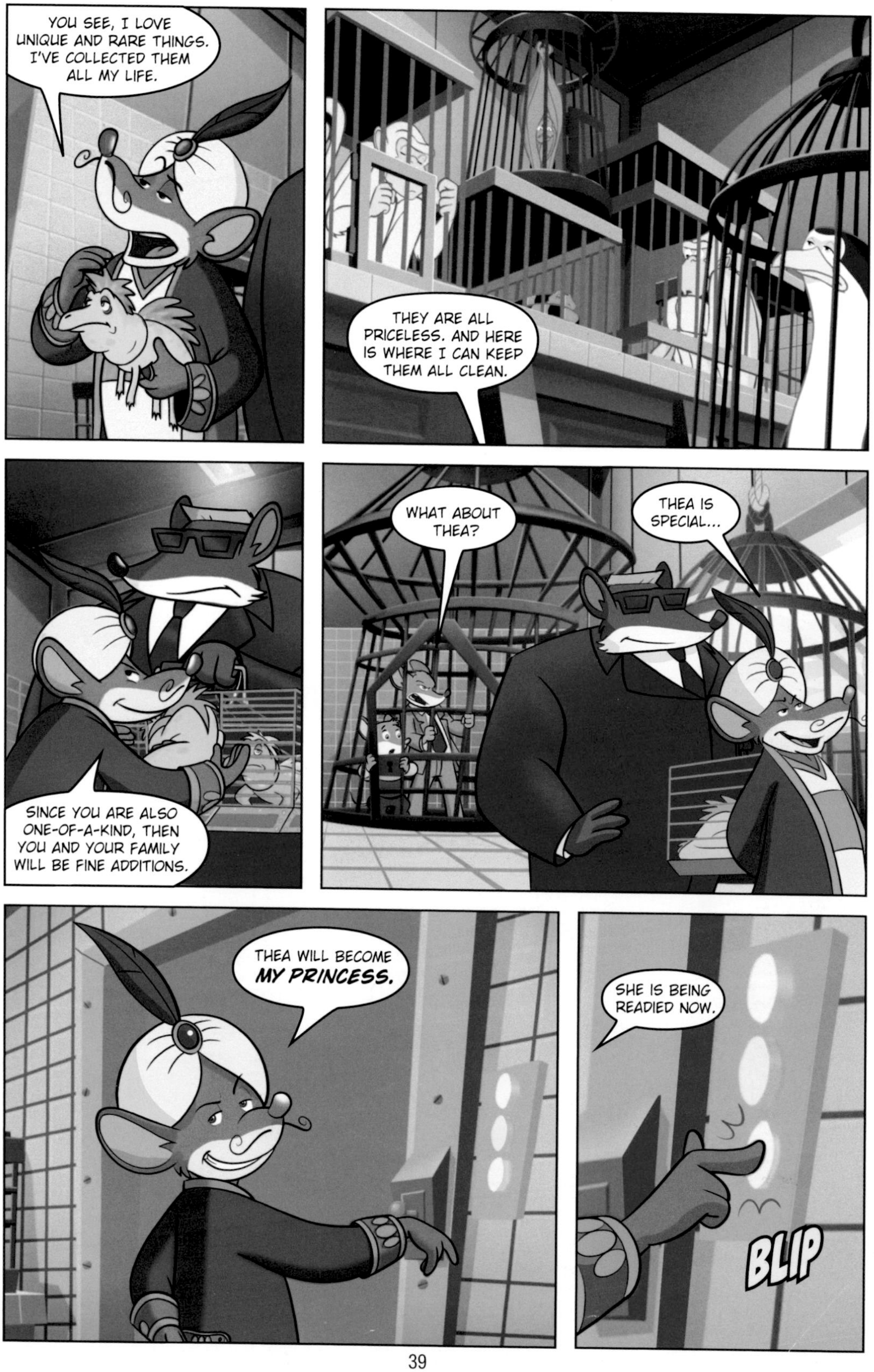
YOU SEE, I LOVE UNIQUE AND RARE THINGS. I'VE COLLECTED THEM ALL MY LIFE.
THEY ARE ALL PRICELESS. AND HERE IS WHERE I CAN KEEP THEM ALL CLEAN.
SINCE YOU ARE ALSO ONE-OF-A-KIND, THEN YOU AND YOUR FAMILY WILL BE FINE ADDITIONS.
WHAT ABOUT THEA?
THEA IS SPECIAL...
THEA WILL BECOME MY PRINCESS.
SHE IS BEING READIED NOW.
BLIP

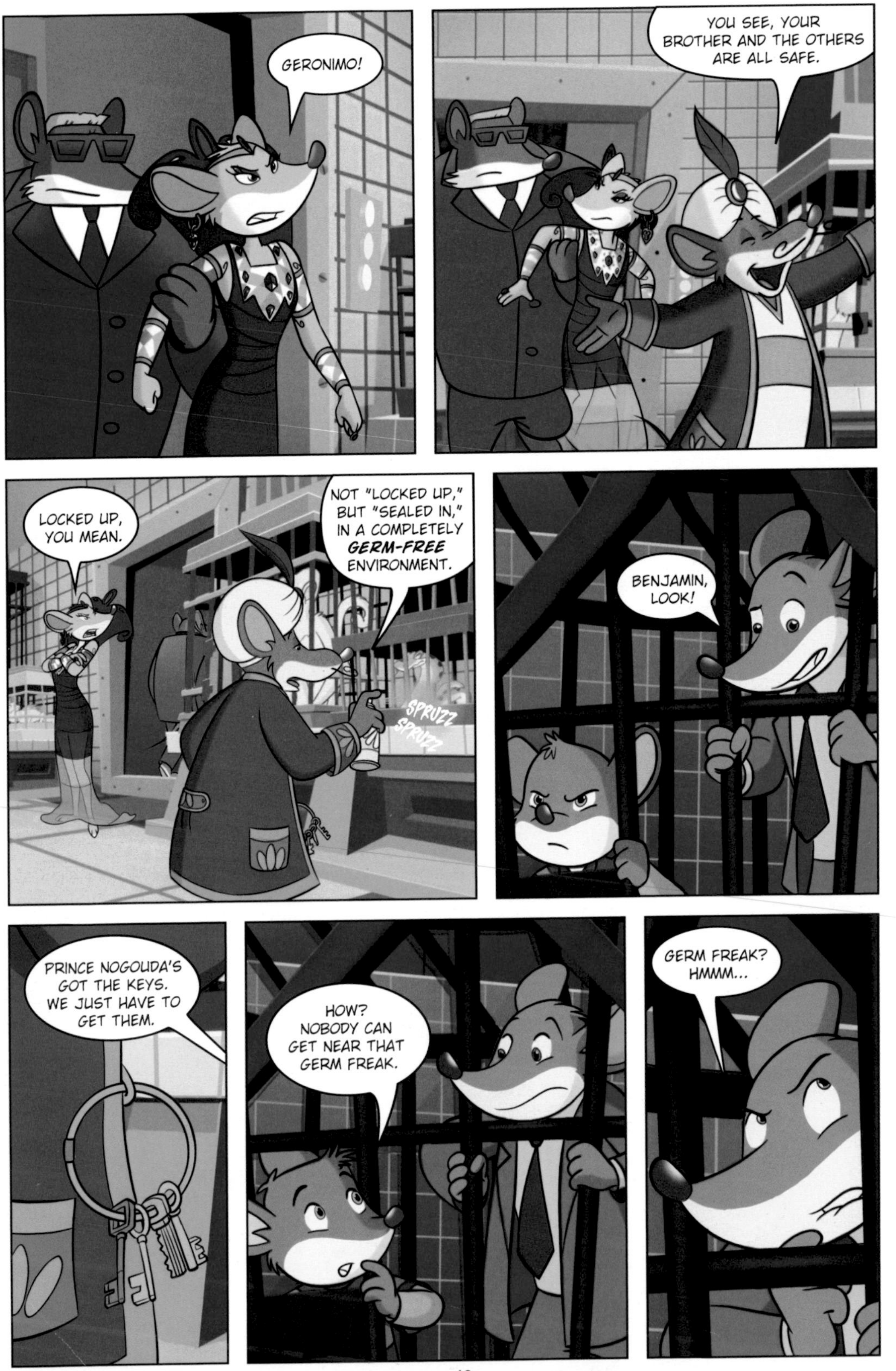
GERONIMO!
YOU SEE, YOUR BROTHER AND THE OTHERS ARE ALL SAFE.
LOCKED UP, YOU MEAN.
NOT "LOCKED UP," BUT "SEALED IN," IN A COMPLETELY **GERM-FREE** ENVIRONMENT.
SPRUZZ SPRUZZ
BENJAMIN, LOOK!
PRINCE NOGOUDA'S GOT THE KEYS. WE JUST HAVE TO GET THEM.
HOW? NOBODY CAN GET NEAR THAT GERM FREAK.
GERM FREAK? HMMM...

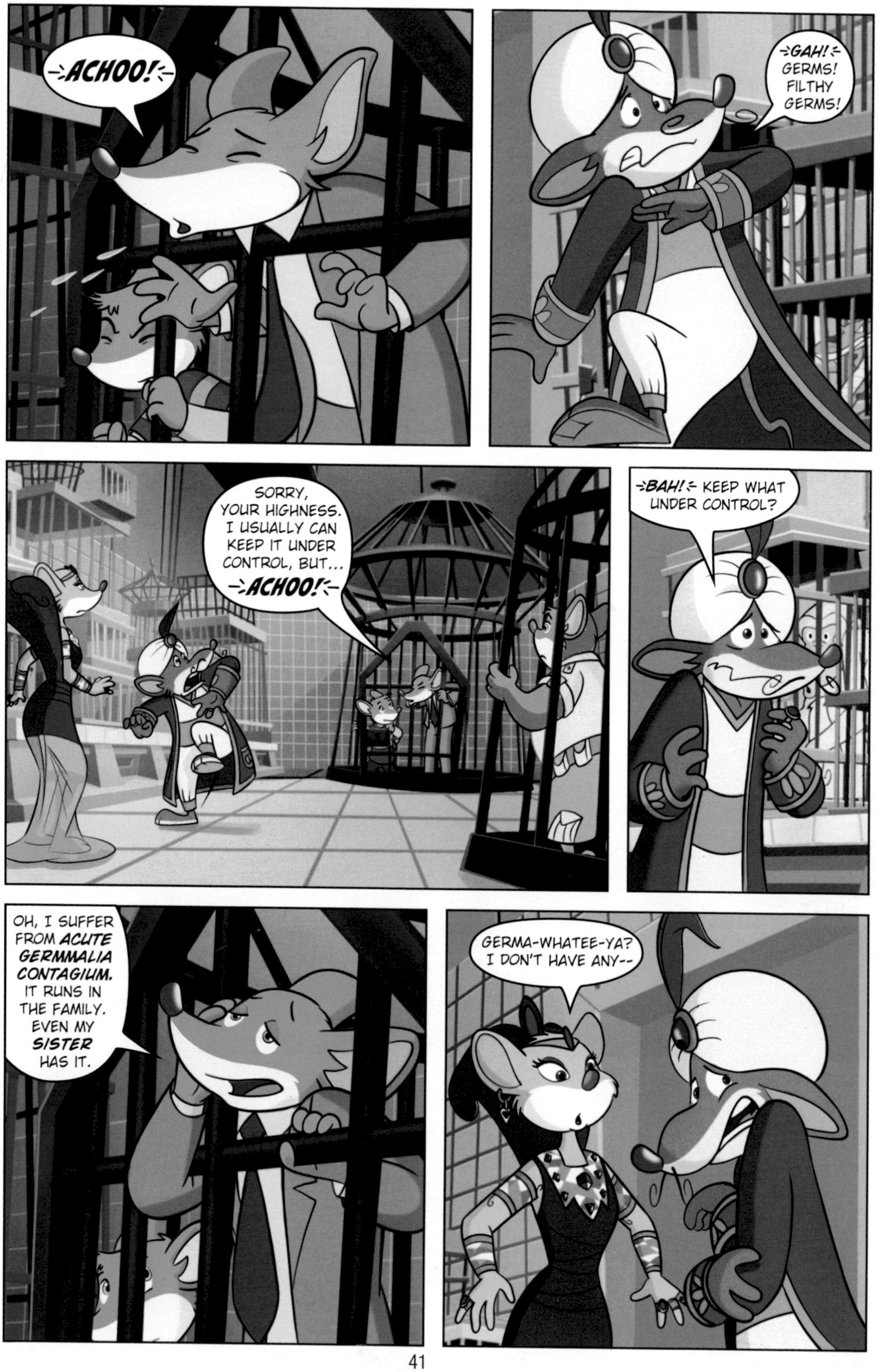
ACHOO!
GAH! GERMS! FILTHY GERMS!
SORRY, YOUR HIGHNESS. I USUALLY CAN KEEP IT UNDER CONTROL, BUT... ACHOO!
BAH! KEEP WHAT UNDER CONTROL?
OH, I SUFFER FROM ACUTE GERMMALIA CONTAGIUM. IT RUNS IN THE FAMILY. EVEN MY SISTER HAS IT.
GERMA-WHATEE-YA? I DON'T HAVE ANY--

OH, RIGHT. GERMA-WHAT-HE-SAID!

ᐳAH·AH·ACHOO!ᐸ

AAAH!

ᐳACHOO!ᐸ

ᐳACHOO!ᐸ

ᐳACHOO!ᐸ

WE HAVE TO GET OUT OF HERE BEFORE WE'RE INFECTED TOO!

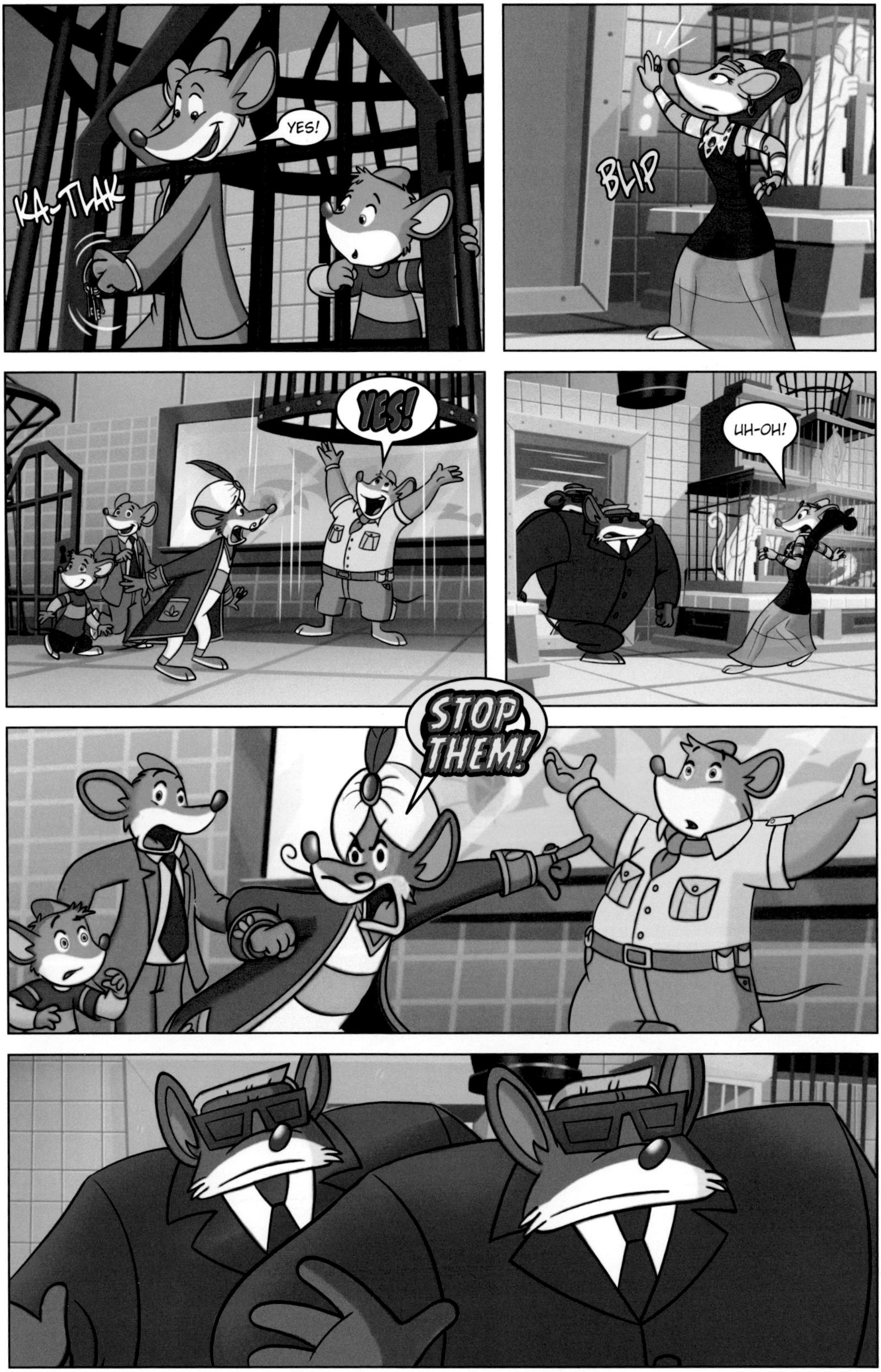
YES!
KA-TLAK
BLIP
YES!
UH-OH!
STOP THEM!

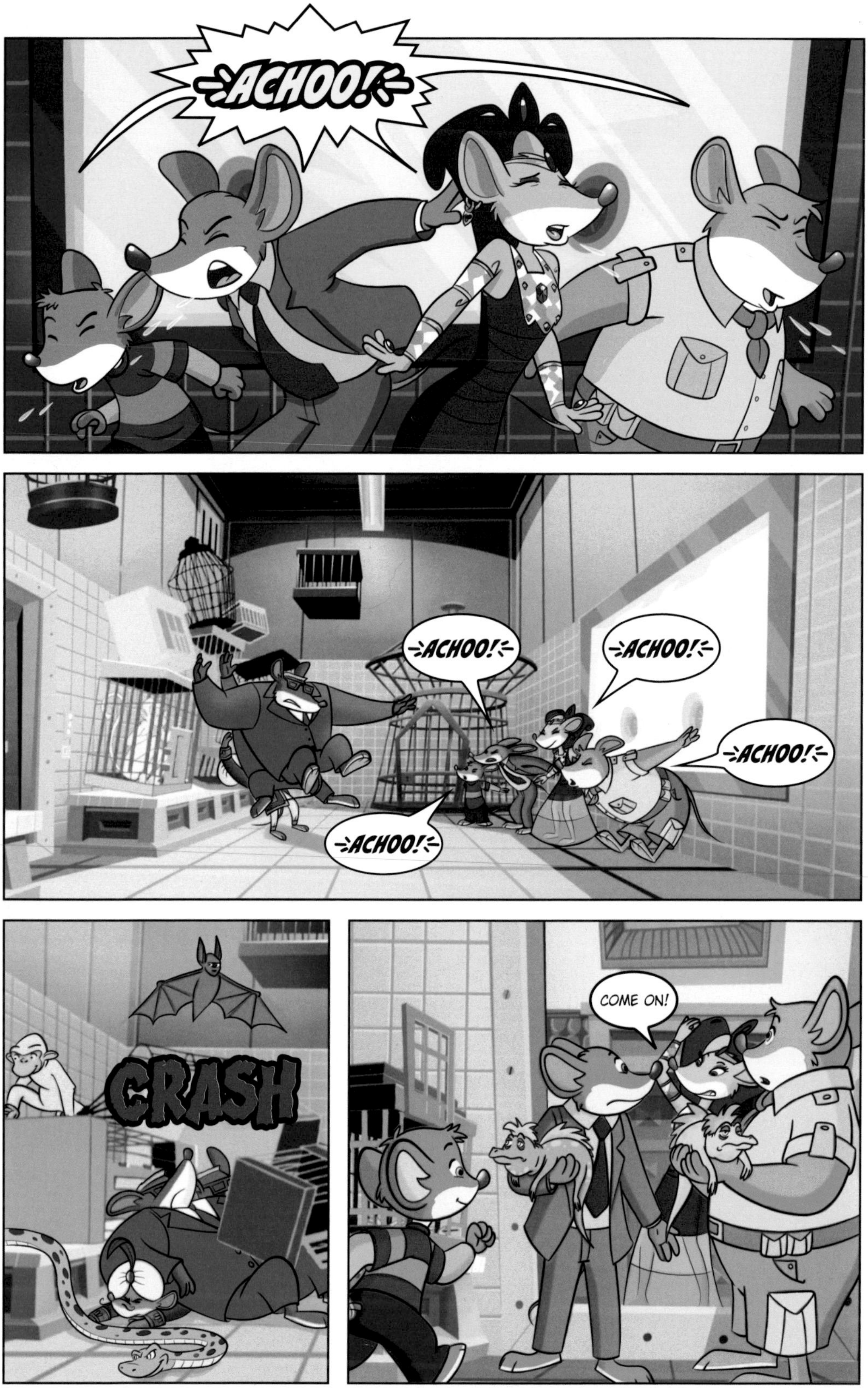
ACHOO!
ACHOO!
ACHOO!
ACHOO!
ACHOO!
CRASH
COME ON!

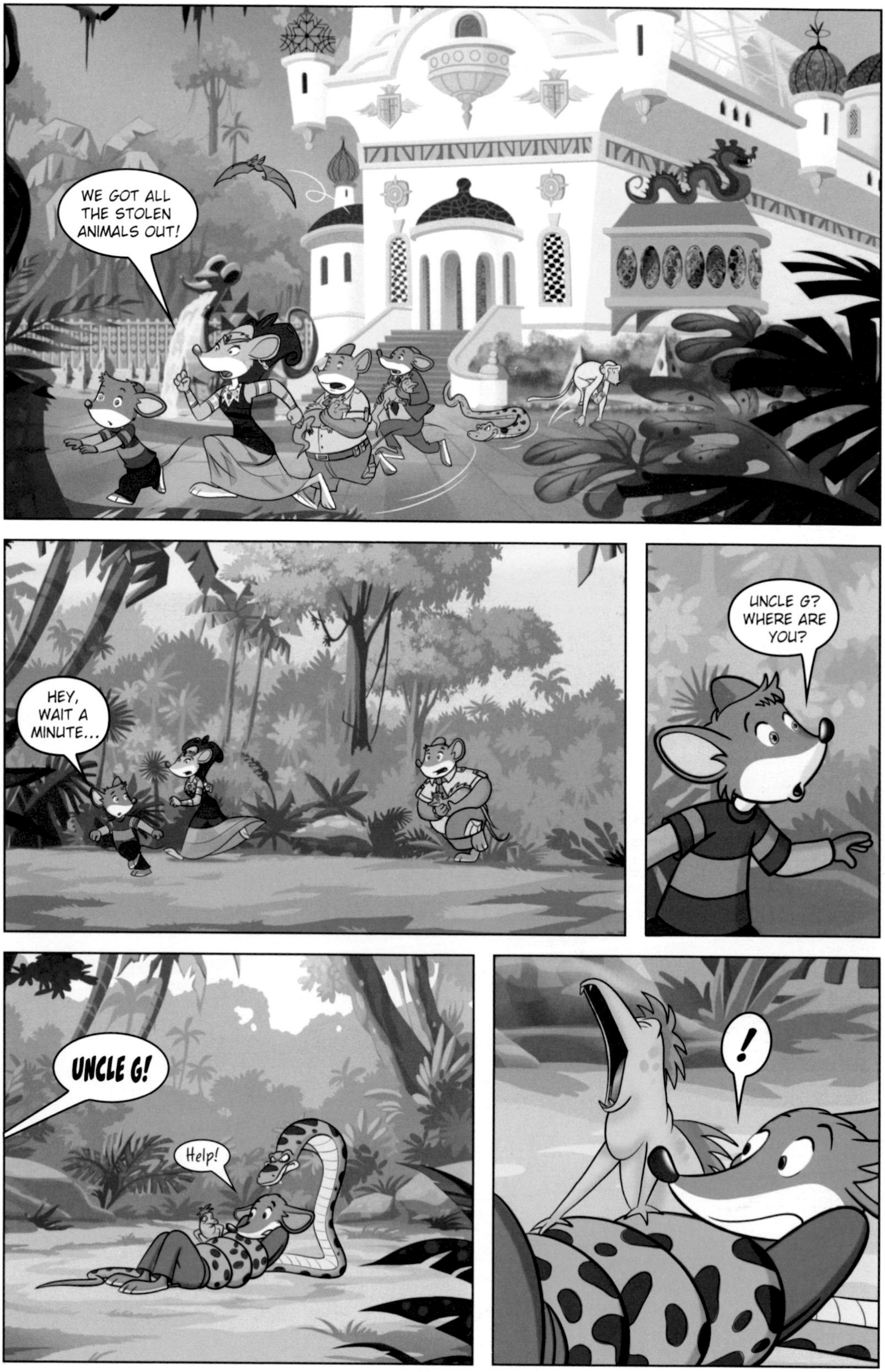
WE GOT ALL THE STOLEN ANIMALS OUT!
HEY, WAIT A MINUTE...
UNCLE G? WHERE ARE YOU?
UNCLE G!
Help!
!

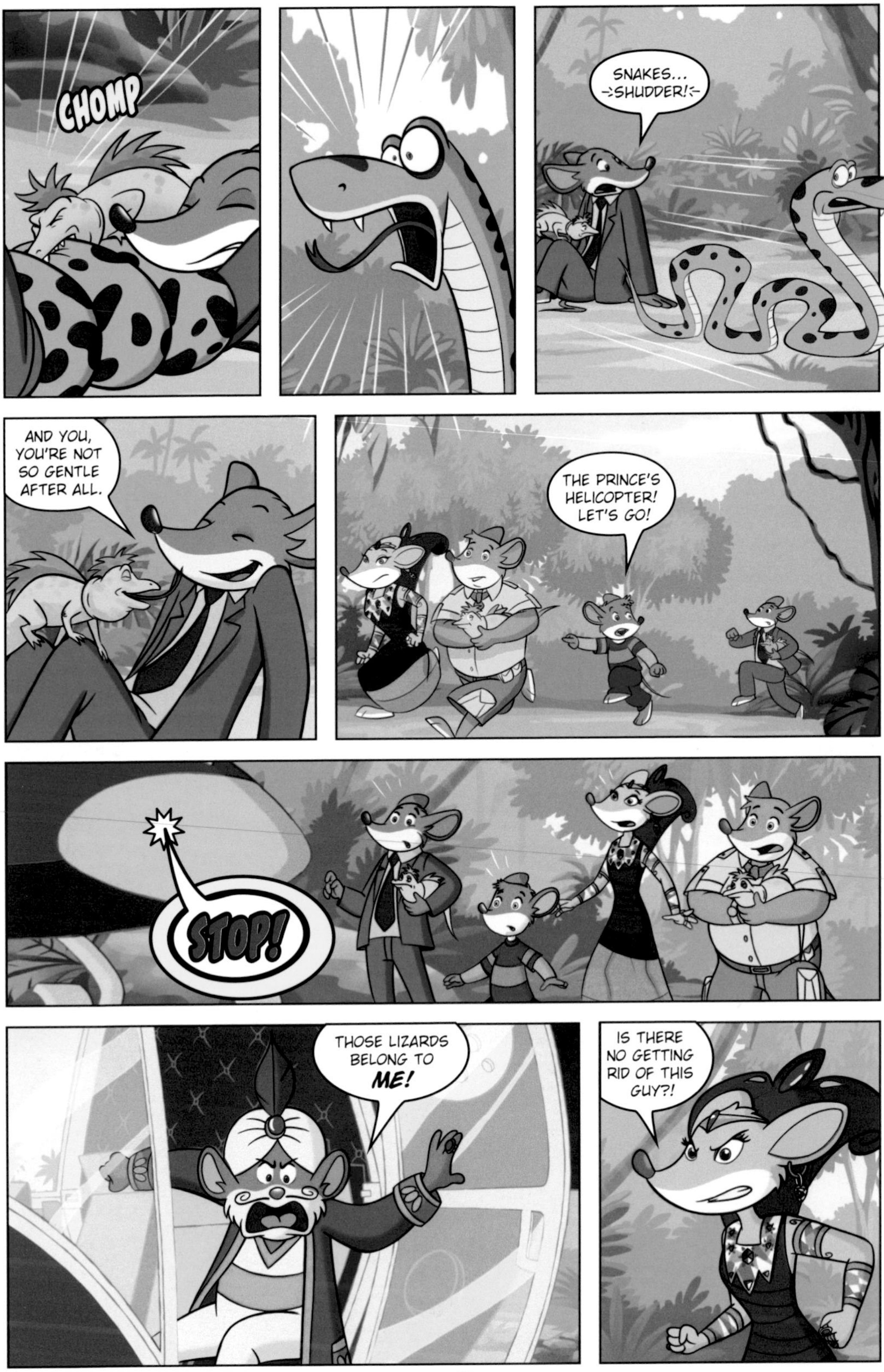
CHOMP
SNAKES... -SHUDDER!-
AND YOU, YOU'RE NOT SO GENTLE AFTER ALL.
THE PRINCE'S HELICOPTER! LET'S GO!
STOP!
THOSE LIZARDS BELONG TO ME!
IS THERE NO GETTING RID OF THIS GUY?!

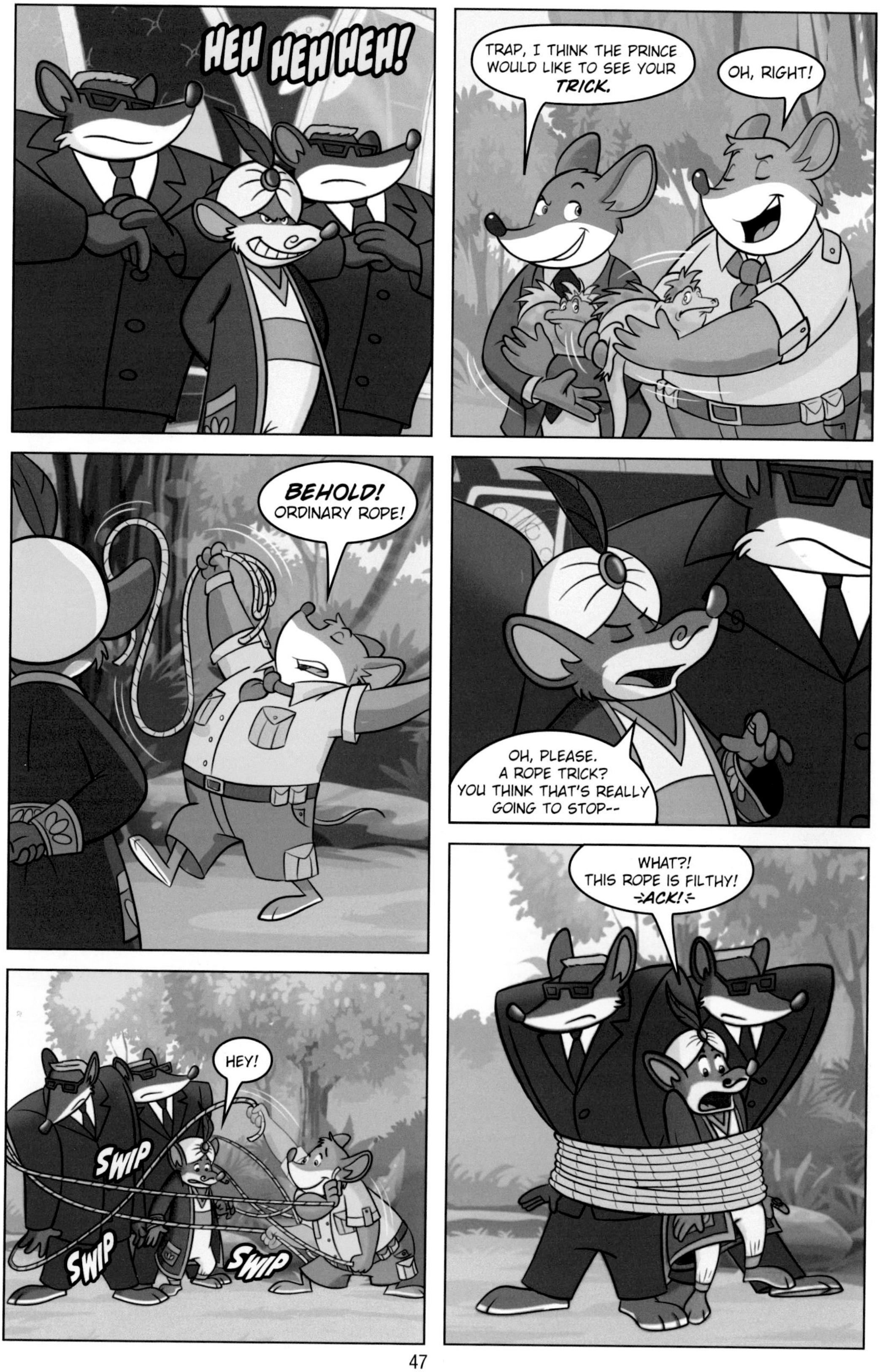
HEH HEH HEH!
TRAP, I THINK THE PRINCE WOULD LIKE TO SEE YOUR TRICK.
OH, RIGHT!
BEHOLD! ORDINARY ROPE!
OH, PLEASE. A ROPE TRICK? YOU THINK THAT'S REALLY GOING TO STOP--
HEY!
SWIP
SWIP
SWIP
WHAT?! THIS ROPE IS FILTHY! ACK!

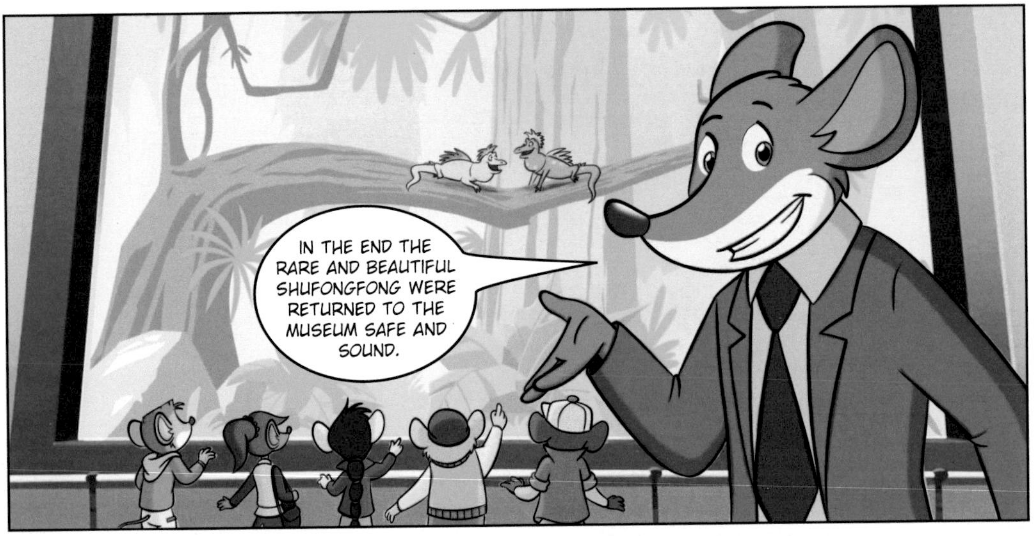
IN THE END THE RARE AND BEAUTIFUL SHUFONGFONG WERE RETURNED TO THE MUSEUM SAFE AND SOUND.

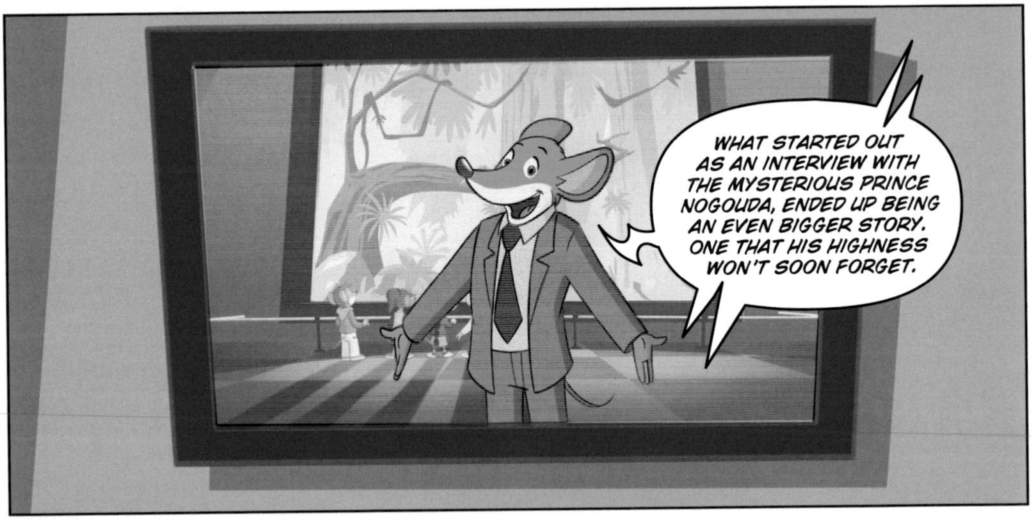
WHAT STARTED OUT AS AN INTERVIEW WITH THE MYSTERIOUS PRINCE NOGOUDA, ENDED UP BEING AN EVEN BIGGER STORY. ONE THAT HIS HIGHNESS WON'T SOON FORGET.

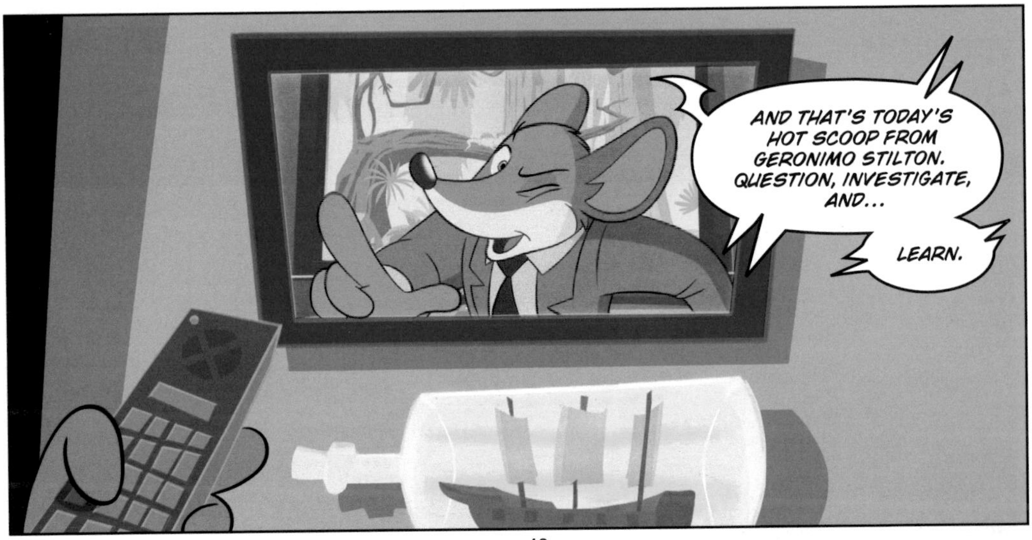
AND THAT'S TODAY'S HOT SCOOP FROM GERONIMO STILTON. QUESTION, INVESTIGATE, AND...
LEARN.

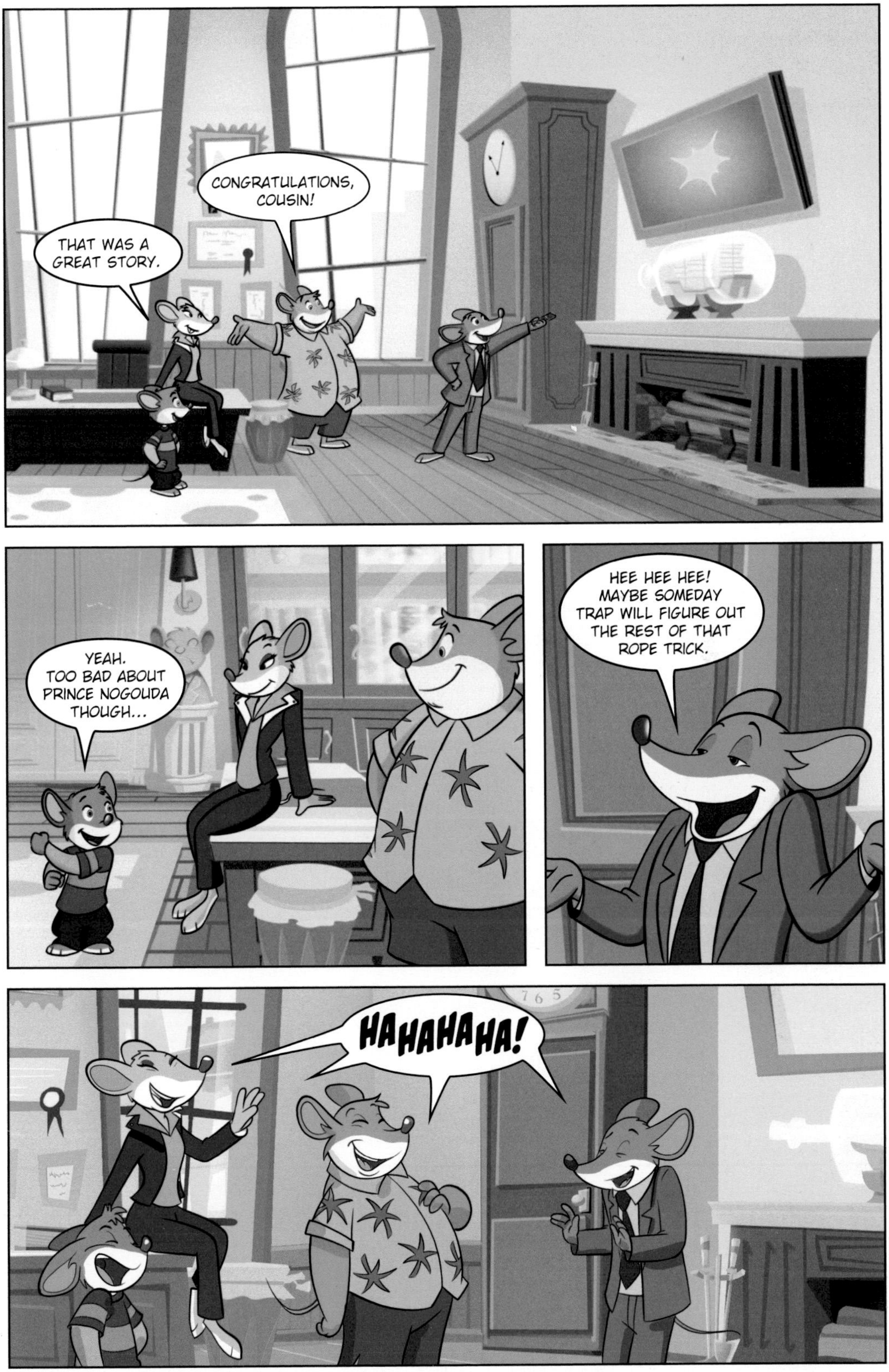
THAT WAS A GREAT STORY.
CONGRATULATIONS, COUSIN!
YEAH. TOO BAD ABOUT PRINCE NOGOUDA THOUGH...
HEE HEE HEE! MAYBE SOMEDAY TRAP WILL FIGURE OUT THE REST OF THAT ROPE TRICK.
HAHAHAHA!

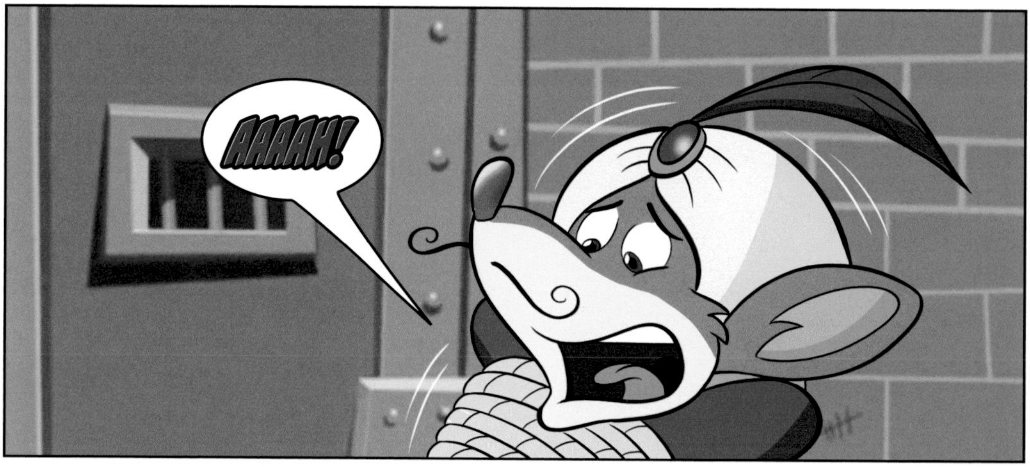
AAAAH!

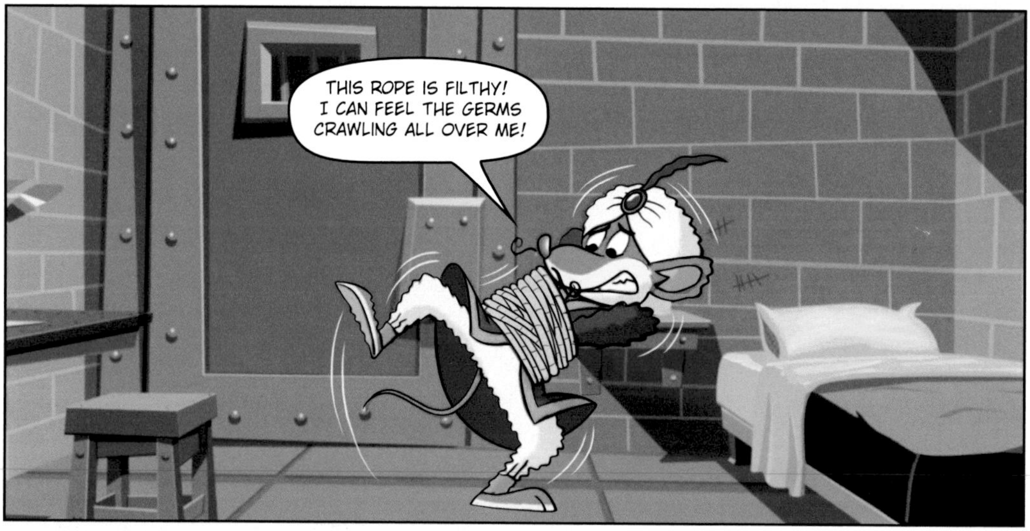
THIS ROPE IS FILTHY! I CAN FEEL THE GERMS CRAWLING ALL OVER ME!

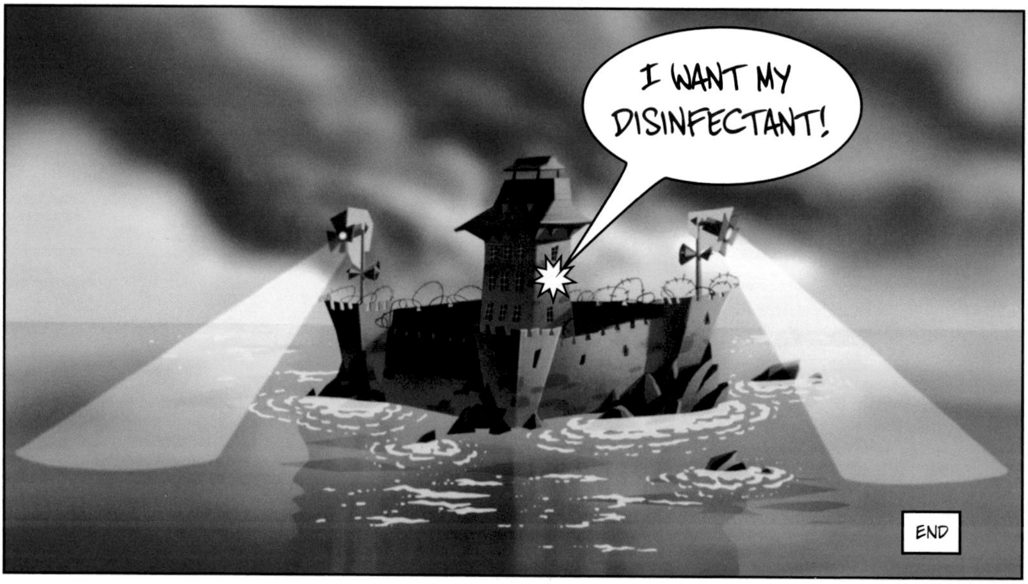
I WANT MY DISINFECTANT!
END

Watch Out For PAPERCUTZ™

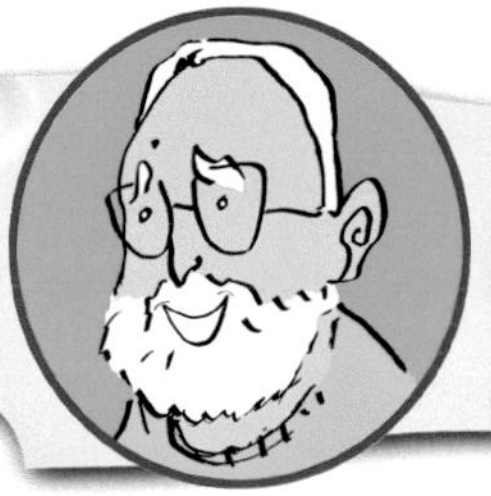

Welcome to the pandemoniac premiere of GERONIMO STILTON REPORTER #1 "Operation Shufongfong," the official graphic novel adaptation of the first animated episode of Geronimo Stilton Season One, written by Julien Frey and Vincent Bonjour, brought to you by Papercutz—those pendantic people dedicated to publishing great graphic novels for all ages. I'm Salicrup, *Jim Salicrup,* the ever-alliterative Editor-in-Chief and used Speedrat salesman.

For those of you who have followed our previous GERONIMO STILTON graphic novels, you may be wondering what's going on here or asking where are the Pirate Cats? Well, fear not, all 19 original GERONIMO STILTON graphic novels are still available from booksellers everywhere, as well as GERONIMO STILTON boxed sets and GERONIMO STILTON 3 IN 1, the new series collecting 3 graphic novels in each volume. What GERONIMO STILTON REPORTER is all about is Geronimo's adventures in the present day. Here's what Geronimo and his friends and family are up to when they're not busy undoing the damage those darn Pirate Cats keep creating in the past. After all, it's hard to run The Rodent's Gazette without actual news in it no matter how exciting Geronimo's historic adventures may be.

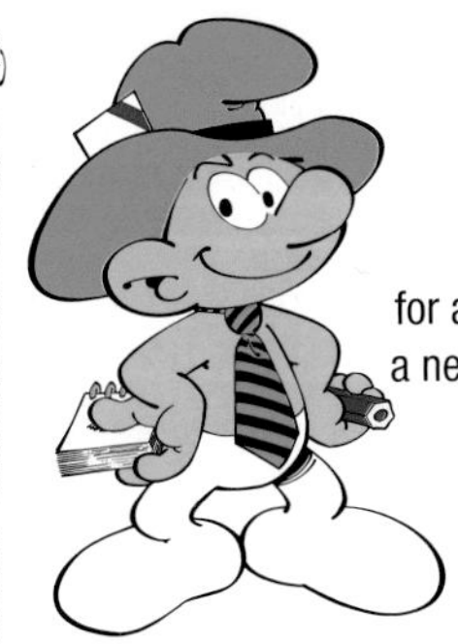

Speaking of newspapers, don't miss THE SMURFS #24 "The Smurf Reporter" graphic novel from Papercutz for a uniquely Smurfy take on how a newspaper gets started and how "Fake News" can come to be. It's virtually a tale torn from today's headlines.

But back to GERONIMO STILTON. In GERONIMO STILTON #18 and #19, we were discussing the Philosophy of GERONIMO STILTON as presented at geronimostilton.com. To be clear, this represents the guidelines for all GERONIMO STILTON stories—the comics, chapter books, and animated TV shows, and also offers an insight into Geronimo's character and motivations. In an age where some folks may believe there's no longer any moral lessons included in today's entertainment for children, we beg to differ, and offer up these excerpts of the Philosophy of GERONIMO STILTON as Exhibit A...

GERONIMO STILTON AND EQUALITY
Geronimo Stilton lives in a multi-cultural society, based on the principles of respecting diversity. Furthermore, Geronimo is very aware of the theme of equality between males and females both in a social and working sense.

While the main goal of each GERONIMO STILTON graphic novel is to entertain, one cannot underestimate the importance of demonstrating through example such values as respecting diversity and equality. In this very volume, Thea Stilton experiences poor treatment from the aptly named Prince Nogouda, who is ultimately punished in the end.

GERONIMO STILTON AND LIFE
Sometimes Geronimo feels as though he's the victim of the unfortunate circumstances he finds himself in. His job absorbs him completely and he feels suffocated by his responsibility to his coworkers, his friends, and his family. But at the end of every adventure Geronimo has the feeling of being in complete harmony with himself and the world, because life is beautiful and he is happy to have so many friends and a family as special as his.

To offer up a little Salicrup Philosophy, the secret to true happiness is to always appreciate what you have. Dwelling on what you don't have will only make you miserable. Geronimo illustrates that point all the time—he loves his friends and family, he loves his work, and he loves life (especially when he feels his is threatened).

But Moldy Mozzarella! Enough philosophizing already! We're here to enjoy GERONIMO STILTON, so on the following pages we present an exclusive partial-preview of GERONIMO STILTON REPORTER #2 "It's MY Scoop!" And be sure to catch Geronimo's animated adventures on NetFlix and Amazon Prime too.

Thanks! JIM

STAY IN TOUCH!

EMAIL:	salicrup@papercutz.com
WEB:	papercutz.com
TWITTER:	@papercutzgn
INSTAGRAM:	@papercutzgn
FACEBOOK:	PAPERCUTZGRAPHICNOVELS
SNAIL MAIL:	Papercutz, 160 Broadway, Suite 700, East Wing, New York, NY 10038

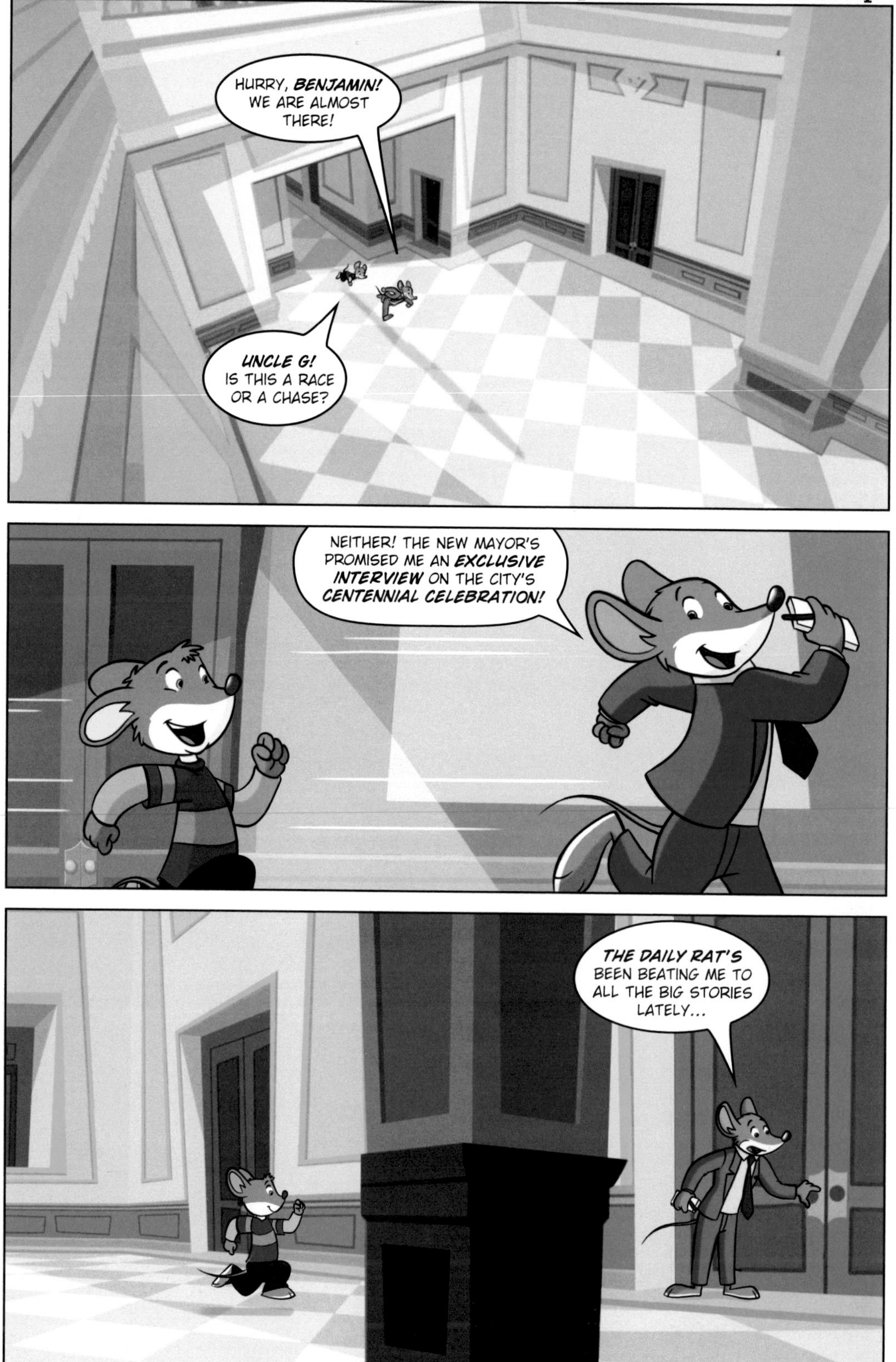
HURRY, BENJAMIN! WE ARE ALMOST THERE!
UNCLE G! IS THIS A RACE OR A CHASE?
NEITHER! THE NEW MAYOR'S PROMISED ME AN EXCLUSIVE INTERVIEW ON THE CITY'S CENTENNIAL CELEBRATION!
THE DAILY RAT'S BEEN BEATING ME TO ALL THE BIG STORIES LATELY...

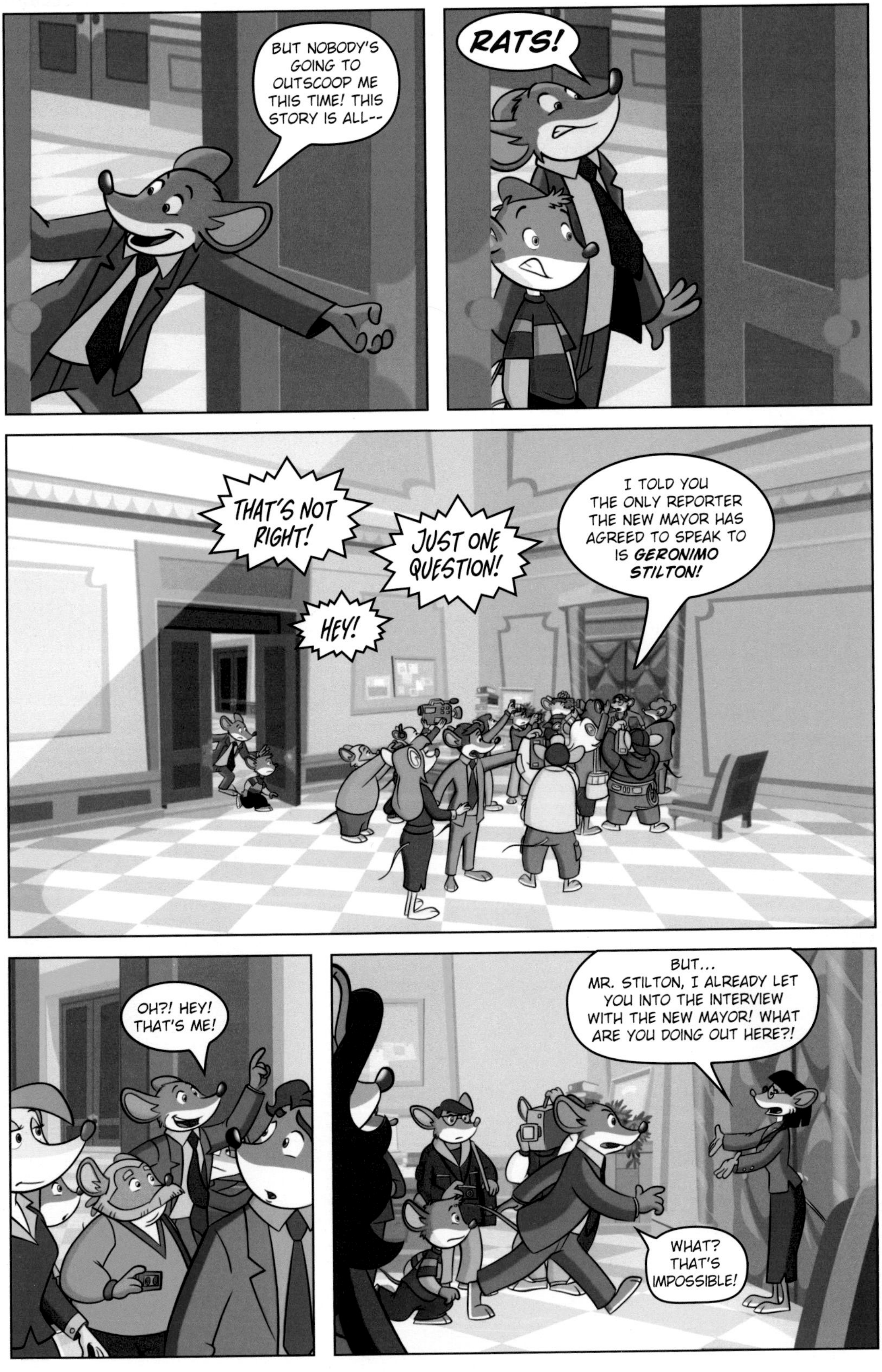
BUT NOBODY'S GOING TO OUTSCOOP ME THIS TIME! THIS STORY IS ALL--
RATS!
THAT'S NOT RIGHT!
JUST ONE QUESTION!
HEY!
I TOLD YOU THE ONLY REPORTER THE NEW MAYOR HAS AGREED TO SPEAK TO IS **GERONIMO STILTON!**
OH?! HEY! THAT'S ME!
BUT... MR. STILTON, I ALREADY LET YOU INTO THE INTERVIEW WITH THE NEW MAYOR! WHAT ARE YOU DOING OUT HERE?!
WHAT? THAT'S IMPOSSIBLE!

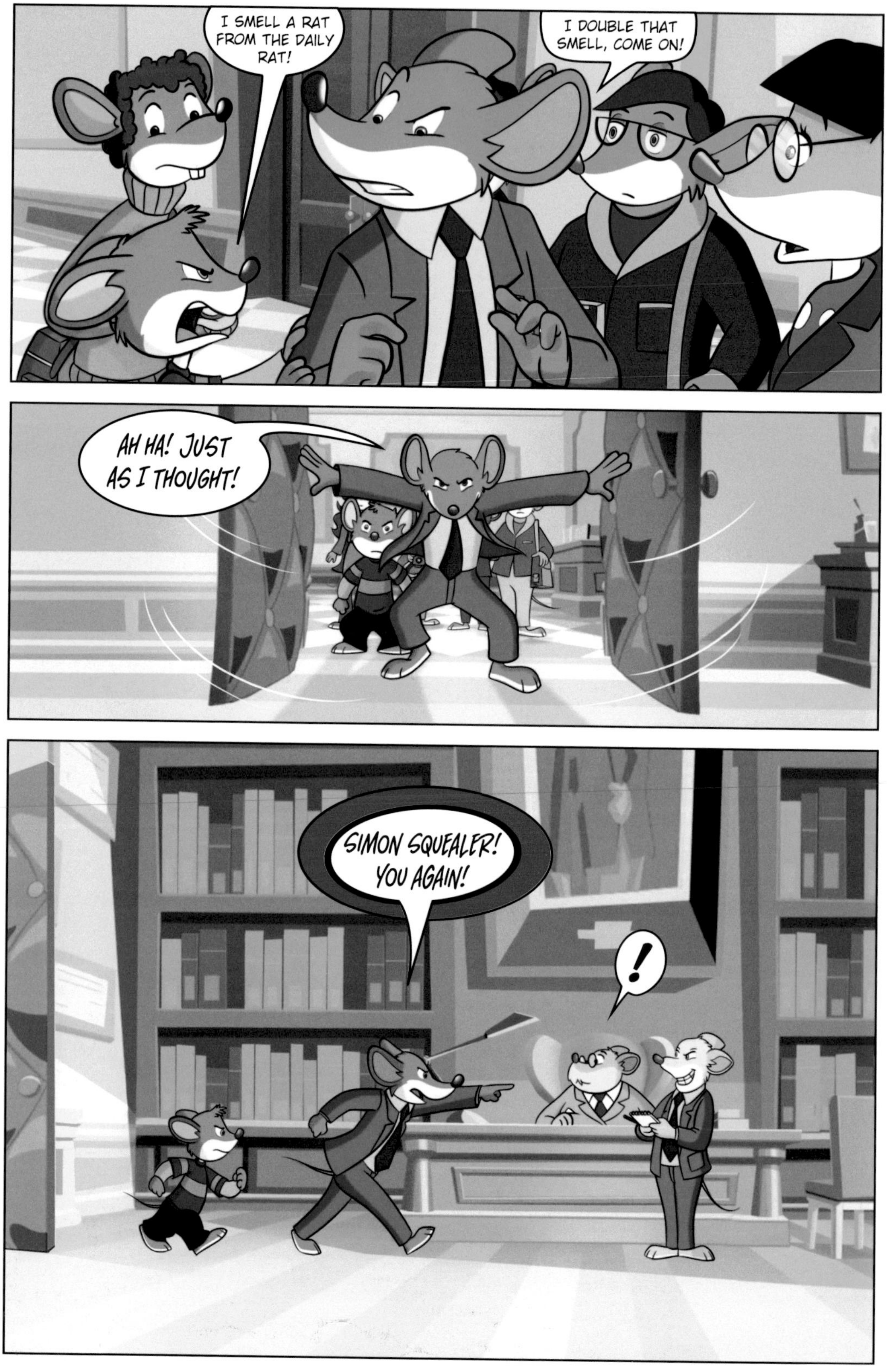
I SMELL A RAT FROM THE DAILY RAT!
I DOUBLE THAT SMELL, COME ON!
AH HA! JUST AS I THOUGHT!
SIMON SQUEALER! YOU AGAIN!
!

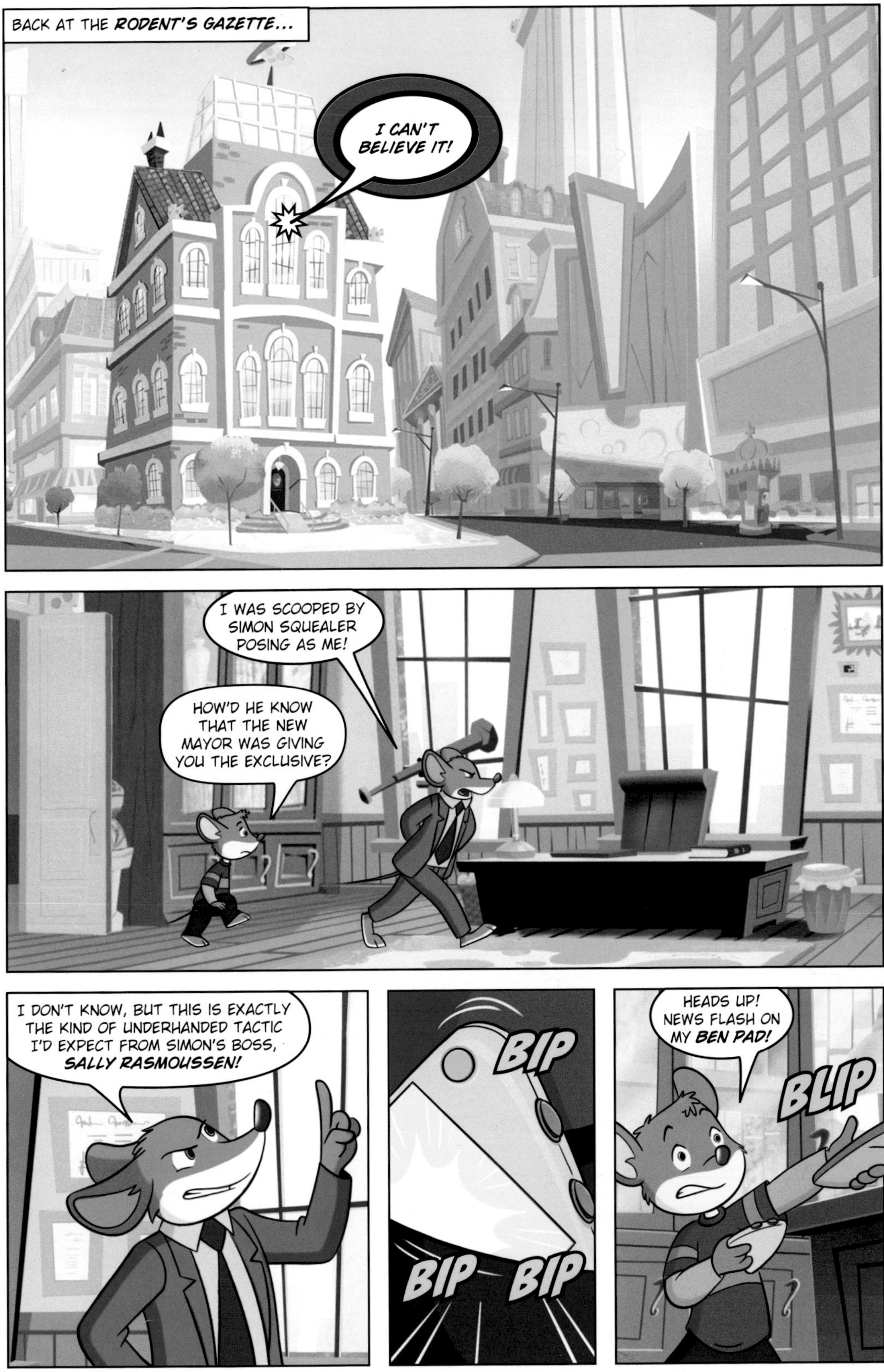
BACK AT THE *RODENT'S GAZETTE...*
I CAN'T BELIEVE IT!
I WAS SCOOPED BY SIMON SQUEALER POSING AS ME!
HOW'D HE KNOW THAT THE NEW MAYOR WAS GIVING YOU THE EXCLUSIVE?
I DON'T KNOW, BUT THIS IS EXACTLY THE KIND OF UNDERHANDED TACTIC I'D EXPECT FROM SIMON'S BOSS, **SALLY RASMOUSSEN!**
BIP
BIP BIP
HEADS UP! NEWS FLASH ON MY **BEN PAD!**
BLIP

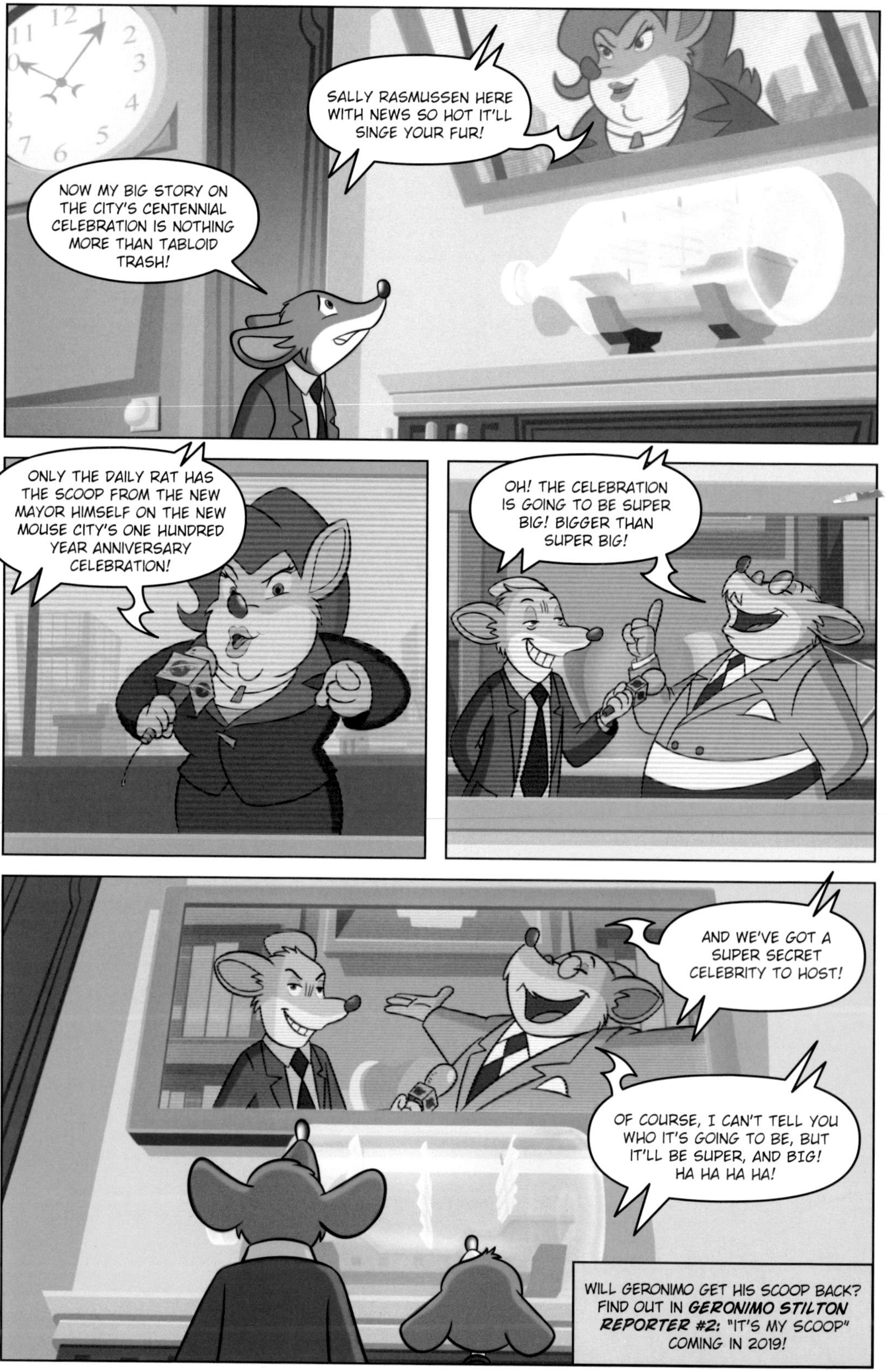
NOW MY BIG STORY ON THE CITY'S CENTENNIAL CELEBRATION IS NOTHING MORE THAN TABLOID TRASH!
SALLY RASMUSSEN HERE WITH NEWS SO HOT IT'LL SINGE YOUR FUR!
ONLY THE DAILY RAT HAS THE SCOOP FROM THE NEW MAYOR HIMSELF ON THE NEW MOUSE CITY'S ONE HUNDRED YEAR ANNIVERSARY CELEBRATION!
OH! THE CELEBRATION IS GOING TO BE SUPER BIG! BIGGER THAN SUPER BIG!
AND WE'VE GOT A SUPER SECRET CELEBRITY TO HOST!
OF COURSE, I CAN'T TELL YOU WHO IT'S GOING TO BE, BUT IT'LL BE SUPER, AND BIG! HA HA HA HA!
WILL GERONIMO GET HIS SCOOP BACK? FIND OUT IN GERONIMO STILTON REPORTER #2: "IT'S MY SCOOP" COMING IN 2019!

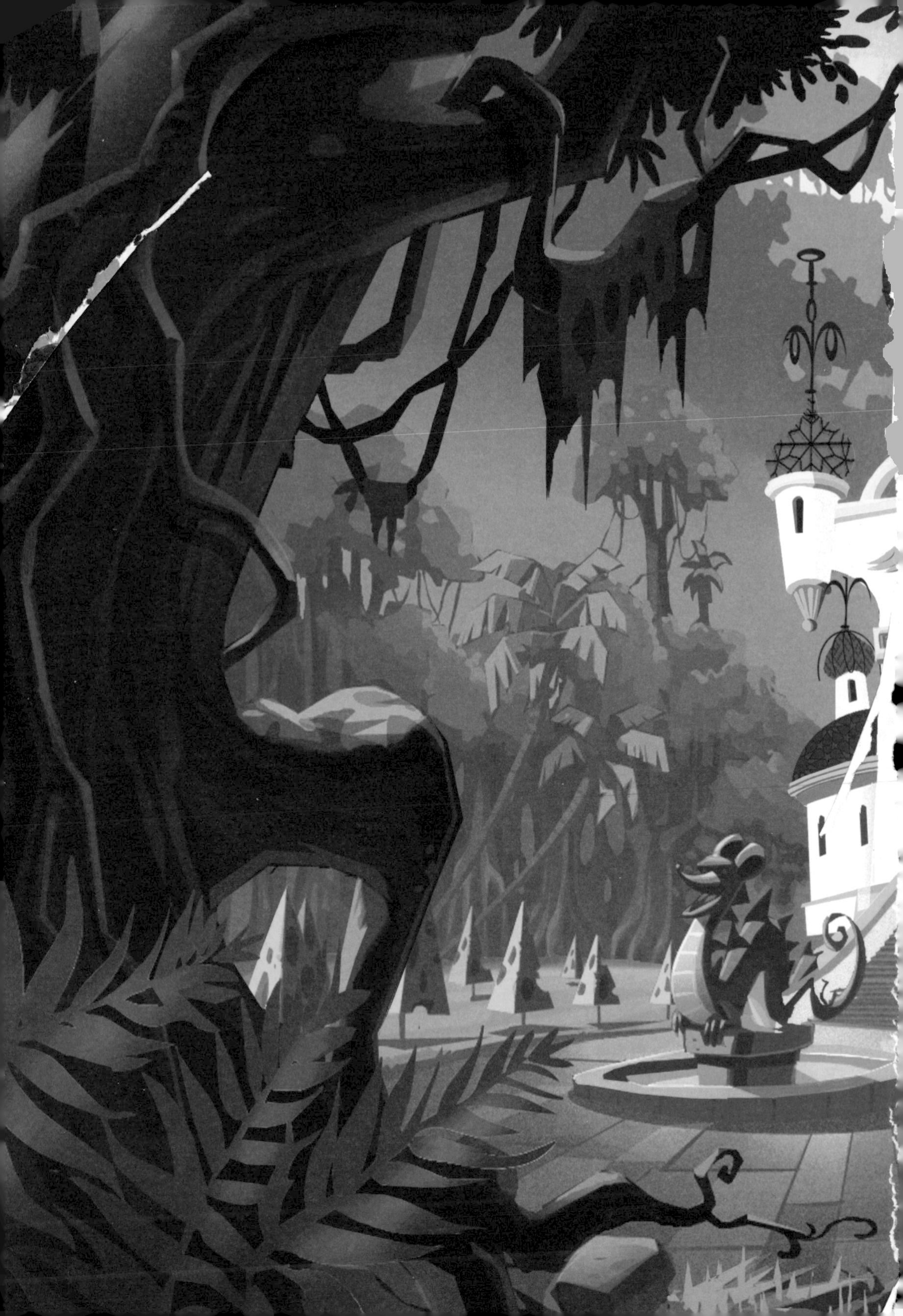